C000050973

MONSTROSITY

LAURA DIAZ DE ARCE

Copyright (C) 2018 Laura Diaz de Arce

Layout design and Copyright (C) 2020 by Next Chapter

Published 2020 by Evenfall – A Next Chapter Imprint

Edited by Kevin Candela

Proofread by Marilyn Wagner

Cover art by Cover Mint

This book is a work of fiction. Names, characters, places, and incidents are the product of the author's imagination or are used fictitiously. Any resemblance to actual events, locales, or persons, living or dead, is purely coincidental.

All rights reserved. No part of this book may be reproduced or transmitted in any form or by any means, electronic or mechanical, including photocopying, recording, or by any information storage and retrieval system, without the author's permission.

*For anyone who was too much
in a world that was not enough.*

CONTENTS

Dear Reader,

When we were children, we dreamed of being heroes. We wanted to slay dragons and defeat the monsters that scared us.

As we grew older, we were forced to try and find our monsters. We had been told they would be easy to spot. Monsters had too many teeth, too much fur, too much size.

These were lies. We stopped wanting to be heroes. We started to want to be more, to be too much. We wanted, needed, more than the world could give us. We wanted more than what we were told we should be. We wanted to become monsters.

Dear Reader, I want three things for you as you read these stories. I hope you find a story that brings you joy. I hope you find a story that gives you some discomfort. Finally, I hope you find a story here that makes you too much, that makes you just a little bit monstrous.

May you be enthralled and entertained by my accounts of monsters. May these stories help you wake up the monster inside.

Laura Diaz de Arce

HOMINUM

WITHOUT HIM (AND HIM, AND HIM) THERE IS NO ME

I COULD SEE THE SMALL IMPERFECTIONS IN HIS BACK tattoos from this angle. One was of a large, grayish dove that circled an oblong skull. The dove's eye was a little off, and I could see its unevenness best as he breathed. His buddy had done that one at the back of a garage. He said it represented how life was short or some such bullshit. They always fed me bullshit, and I ate it up.[1]

The light was coming in high in this piece of shit motel. He was still passed out on the cheap beer and whiskey he'd bought at the gas station last night. I got up and pulled on his shirt.

It reeked of him, his dried sweat, spilled beer and the dust of the desert. Just yesterday, I'd found that smell attractive, but it was losing its luster. Now it smelled like distaste, a gross substitute for a body melting in front of me.

I knew he liked it when I looked like this. When he would wake up, he'd find me in his worn shirt, my eyeliner from last night smudged in the right way, my hair half out and teased and a lit cigarette hanging out my mouth at an angle. He'd look at me, without a second thought, but I know that if I give him that bitch-tired look, he can't stop his dick from twitching. We have a lot in common, he and I, we both like to feel like shit.

He'll probably pull me on top of him and we'll fuck. It wouldn't be lovemaking, that's not what I'd call it. No, we'd rut like animals for a few minutes. He won't wait for me to get wet, he'll just jam his hands between my thighs, pushing his calloused fingers into my skin to pull them apart. He thinks his roughness is hot. He gives himself too much credit. My cheeks will burn, not from flush but from the wire of his beard as he pushes his tongue down my throat. He'll grab my tits, not to titillate me, but for his own amusement. Then he'll jam his withering half-hard dick into me and I'll have to force out a convincing moan, not that he needs convincing.

A few days ago, that would have been the thing that kept me. I'd feel fulfilled for a few moments, warm in the embrace, in the attention, in the knowledge that I'd won the game. But that's not me today. Today it feels like it's going to be a chore. And this life, that I had hoped wouldn't be routine, has its own slow, stupid rhythm. And now I'm getting bored, just like with the rest of them.

We'd met four months ago in a small, no-name hole north of Reno, but he followed a string of my lovers. Men. I need to taste new flavors and I crave the ones I've yet to taste. I'll play with the flavor on my tongue, but soon the taste is bland and burnt. I look to taste men to fit my moods.

* * *

I started out, like most people did, with Vanilla. Not even regular vanilla, vanilla sweetened with Splenda. He was a homegrown, good old boy. The captain of our football team with me, the homecoming queen. Small town clichés. He'd pray apologies to Jesus after we made out. I wanted more, but all he'd let me get away with was a nervous teenage hand job once in a while. He smelled like wet grass and sweat from team practice. I still see his perfect teeth, his dimpled chin. His fake masculinity and confidence was the gross aftershave left in a closed-mouthed kiss. When I was with him, I wore knee-length skirts and cardigan sweaters to prayer group. As prom queen, I learned to smile prettily to hide my disinterest.

After a messy breakup with my football captain that included him crying at my front door, threatening suicide, I moved on to the class clown. He had the pop and lightness of Ginger Ale. His freckles dotted his face and body down straight to his pelvis. He was skinny and bare chested, with those same freckles dotting his shoulders and torso. The head of his circumcised dick had a solitary freckle on the tip that I first thought was cute, but became an obnoxious blemish. He smelled like weed, deodorant and fabric freshener.

I wore loose jeans, dark t-shirts and crooked eyeliner to get his attention. I let my hair get greasy and taught myself to smoke weed when I set my eyes on him. He was on the scent like I was a bitch in heat before the week was out. His jokes and his moves (a total of five) got stale. But with him I got to play it as one of the guys. I was cool, I was funny and low maintenance.

The performance was draining.

And then there was Chocolate, he was an aspiring designer or some nonsense. We went to a lot of clubs, a lot of parties where he bullshitted his talent and his business prowess. I was the in-person model that he showed off like the latest phone.

He put me in skin-tight jeans and dresses with slits up the side. I pranced in heels that I had to abuse myself to walk in. And he fucked me, with eyes open so wide it looked like it hurt.

When I smell strong cologne or hear the heavy bass of a rap song, I think of him.

It was Chocolate's investor that took me on. He liked fine things and he had the money to get those things. It wasn't his money that bought me as a mistress. It was the way he looked at me over a glass of overpriced scotch. Like I was already his.

I was.

He was older, married and in his forties, but he looked good. He had the chiseled and styled features of a well-kept vintage. He tasted like leather, cigars and old Hollywood. He kept me in furs and tailored wear.

We'd cruise to some event with me on his arm, a starlet's smile on my lips and a long cigarette on my fingertips. I was a trophy for him too. I'd prance and slither like a charming sex kitten, hidden in silk. He didn't need to tell me, he wanted other men to want me. He wanted them to covet his property, his car, his clothes, his money and his mistress.

I was a seductive flirt to every man we met. From the balding business partners to the young, hot muscular waiters. Their eyes would focus first on my lashes, then creep slowly down to my lined and plumped lips, then continue on down to my breasts. When they got there, I'd time a breath to heave them up and down, the exhalation directing them lower still. And when they reached my waist, I'd shift my weight from one foot to the other so that my hips swayed from one side to the other.

The message was clear: Imagine this young body writhing beneath you. Imagine the kind of man you could be. I was a living fantasy for the wolves. And if he saw them watching me, saw them scouting his object, he'd get hot for me.

Looking back, the sex was dull. He was only into foreplay if it subdued me. But all I needed was the memory of those eyes on me, of the hungry stares that ate me up. That filled me with a delicious, caramel flavored warmth. Rich, sweet, bad for you.

We traveled, a lot. Hopping from one glittering city to

another and staying in penthouses, each one a gilded cage where I was on display. I learned to fix cocktails and do my nails quietly. I learned to subtly hint that I needed money for things and in some ways, it was bliss. He was strong in a way I wasn't, in a way that didn't care for people or consequences.

I didn't want to leave, but his wife caught up with us in Miami and chased me out.

The newspapers never got him right. The headlines read "Tragic Murder-Suicide: Heiress Kills Husband and Self After Going Broke." She killed the love of my life. Sometimes I think maybe she should have taken me too. Our death would have been so artistic. So beautiful with my young beautiful body bleeding out with his refined older one.

* * *

Las Vegas made me feel like an empty soda pop bottle.

The men there were as empty as me, none could give me what I needed as I hollowed my day down the strip. The artificial scent they pumped through casinos, the cheap buffets and fake jewelry, the vapid heat that made the sweat disappear from your brow before it forms made me sick. The most sickening was the cloud of complimentary bathroom perfume that choked the air like a sunken cloud.

I was sick.

I was empty.

Then I saw them.

They drove by in their bikes clad in leather. Driving though the strip like they owned the place, and suddenly I was hungry again.

How self-assured they were, a pack of animals prowling for what they wanted. I could smell it, the oily tar from cigarettes and gas fumes. It all cut through the pristine casino and hotel lobbies. It hacked away at the artificially perfumed air, the cologne and the buffets like a machete. I wanted one. I needed one. I wanted to ride those bikes to the desert. I wanted to fuck and be fucked.

I wanted the older, leathered skin to contrast against my tight young body.

The ride was nice but Reno turned out to be suburban hell. Fortunately, just a few miles and bottles West, there was a little Piece-of-Shit half city with all the essentials: a strip club, three bars, two tattoo parlors and a Walmart. It was like their breeding ground.

My first stop was the tattoo parlor. My skin, despite everything, had remained virginal.

Would I bleed for one of them?

Yes. Yes, I would.

"Fresh meat," one of them growled as I walked in. You could see in my shorts and my top didn't cover much, it was obvious nothing had been inked before. It was cute, like he was trying to scare me. It took most of my control not to laugh and bark at him.

I just winked at the one with ink and he was putty.

By the end I had "Margaret" tattooed on my shoulder and two other obvious pieces done.

"Why Margaret?" he asked, dipping the needle into the pot.

"It was my grandmother's name," I lied. I just like that name.

He finished the belladonna flower on my inside thigh the next afternoon.

And I finished him, because I had no money.

I didn't stay because he didn't have a bike.

* * *

This one I found when the pieces came together.

The Licorice that is fucking me in this cheap motel. I saw him across the room in one of those bars in that little shithole place. I had my trap set and he was like a fly to the spider, with my torn stockings, fraying shorts and stolen leather jacket. My cheap, poorly drawn drugstore makeup and boxed dye just screamed "Daddy Issues" and he was hooked. He bought me a shot, and then four and then a ride to the closest motel.

He smelled like beer, but that was fine.

He was the heat of summer, an unconcerned, unwavering, and unsympathetic summer. He was who he knew he was: a man in his early fifties still pushing drugs as a means to shift from place to place. A man with fierce loyalty to his buddies and his own set of issues set in stone.

Or he *was*.

Now I think he's too old to be pushing drugs like he did at that age. And his buddies are fine, I guess, but not worth his sense of loyalty.

What I loved most about him was his bike.

The other love in his life. It wasn't just a machine. It was an experience. On the road I felt like the me I should be. Every moment racing on the open road felt like flight. I'd let the wind cut between my open fingers and the kicked-up dirt get tangled in my hair. It smelled like gasoline and freedom.

It's late in the afternoon and I make the excuse to go to the ice machine. At the back of the motel I steal a cigarette. Here there's a flimsy wire fence that divides us from the desert. I look out to that landscape and I can breathe. It's void and yet beautiful. It exists for itself, for its emptiness. Sure, there are the shrubs, the rock and desert critters, the odd, random pieces of trash but they only make the quiet louder. It's got a hell of a palette that we paint on its surface with our bike tracks. It's a place impermanently marked by our footsteps. Eventually the wind comes and blows over those steps making it new. The desert's changes are makeup, wiped away to reveal the skin of it.

There's that bright blue sky, that golden ocean of sand and I realize I'm miserable. He kept my attention for a bit, but the sweet taste is gone. I've got to find a way to ditch him.

The little hotel corner market has dry shampoo and powdered flea insecticide of all things and I start to hatch a plan to get rid of him but keep the bike. As much as I don't like him, I love the power of that machine between my legs. I pick them up in cash and head back to the hotel. He's got a stash he only uses for himself, it's not for sale. It's for us, when we want, but I never partake. I tell him it'll ruin my figure, and "baby, you're all the drug I need".

He's in the shower when I cut the stash.

And I wait.

* * *

Two days later and he's finally feeling it.

We're riding on his bike in a lonely stretch of desert. The bike starts wobbling and he pulls over to the side and starts retching behind a fallen road sign. Out here, we're alone and I'm thankful. It couldn't be better. I'd hoped he'd just get sick enough to have an ER pick him up somewhere and keep him out of my hair.

"Give me a sec babe, I need to sit for a bit," he says, looking like death.

He's pale, and old.

So old.

I hold my breath and touch his forehead. He responds by puking next to my boots. A little bit of vomit dots the black toe and I hold my temper to keep from socking him. "Baby, you've got a fever." I don't really know if he does, but I'm sure he thinks he does.

"Our cell doesn't have any bars." It does but I know he won't check as his eyes are glazing over with illness.

"Give me the keys baby, I'll get help."

And he looks up at me, weak. Gross. He looks like a wounded animal, like a raccoon that's been run over but isn't quite dead yet, just suffering. If I had a gun, I would put him out of his misery.

He hands me the keys. So trusting. I blow him a kiss and drive off on the bike he only started to teach me to ride a few weeks ago. It feels lighter than I remember. I look out at the sunset and turn in that direction.

And it's just me, the road, and the desert.

And I'm free.

Free like the expanse of it.

But I think about him for a minute after I leave.

Maybe someone will find him and get him help.

Maybe he'll die and the sand will cover his body as he disappears into the landscape.

The desert righting itself.

That thought fills me with an inexplicable calm, and then I think, maybe I should head to San Francisco. Maybe catch me a Silicon Valley mogul.

THREE BEATS PER MEASURE

I DO NOT REMEMBER THOSE HOURS. I CANNOT TELL YOU what happened, it is a black spot in my memory, but I remember what caused it. I know it was my fault because I made myself this way. I made myself this way because I had no choice.

They say these things come from the parents, but I do not think that is the truth. My parents, they did not have what I had. We were nothing alike, or at least I thought we were nothing alike. Mama and Papa were the cool of freshly frozen ice. Even in the most excitable of situations, they were calm. I ran hot. As a toddler I did not learn to walk, I ran. I did not learn to coo and speak, I screamed. I did not play, I waged destruction. My parents' lives, while I was a youth, were clouded by my screams, my fits, my rages. It is I who put them off having other children, a fact they made clear to me in the most temperate of voices.

My childhood is filled with the memories of their attempts to tame my nature. Mama especially tired herself out in the endeavor. They put me in structured activities to find a way for me to channel my energy elsewhere. These activities and lessons did nothing to sedate me: soccer, martial arts, violin, tennis, piano, etc. These activities only gave me more fuel with which to torment them.

They tried to train my body to be less of itself. For instance, during meals I was strapped to a chair to make me stop fidgeting. I remember the coolness of my mother's fingers as she slipped the straps beneath my armpits. She was delicate, but not in a way that was concerned for my well-being. A withering presence was her nature; a nature that, looking back, I finally realized had been constructed to hide something else.

Our battles came to a head on the morning of my first period. Until then I only knew that I had an energy, a fire within. I did not have a name for it; not even when it made my face flush and my pulse race. That was that day that I came to know it, as the blood trickled down my inner thigh. There was not much, I was only thirteen, but the glide of that droplet queued something instinctual.

Rage. That was the heat beneath my skin. Anger so fine, so woven into my being that I knew that it was unnatural. This rage. This monster that slithered beneath me. That day I slammed a chair through our sliding glass door. I remember it shattering, the sound of it, the way the shards rained down like snow. There was not a scratch on me, my anger making me impenetrable. Who I was angry at, or for what, I cannot say.

When I did that, when the glass door was shattered and revealed my nature, I could have sworn I saw it. In my mother's eyes, blue eyes that rarely flinched, was a spark of that same anger. Now that I think about it, the rage that resided in my being was perhaps something I had inherited. But she, she must have learned to control it at a young age; restrict it, coat it in clay, dirt and ice such that you would not know what simmered just below the surface.

Eventually, I learned to hide it, at least to a degree. Still it ran like lava through me. I was always conscious of the monster inside. Beneath every disarming smile, coquettish laugh or downward-cast eye, it lay in wait, chomping at the bit. Like my mother, I thought I had it under control.

After a time, I went to University, and then off to a career in a distant and cold city. I had hoped the cold of this place would keep it hibernated. Things were smooth for a while, I did not think of it, of the anger pulsing in my being at every moment. My days were filled with work, with the everyday: picking up groceries, going to my job, keeping appointments. My anger would leap up at times, causing a tremor in my hands or a redness to my face. I could quell these bursts and it was fine. I was alone, but I was fine. I was surviving.

That is, until I received the call.

The police took months to conclude their investigation, in part because they had difficulty putting my father's body together. They did not even fully identify him until they had peeled portions of his face off the kitchen cabinets. Locals from a small town, the police had never seen such carnage and they needed to bring in forensic experts to recreate the crime.

For weeks after, newspapers questioned and sensational-ized what my mother had done. They were incredulous, for how could a small, quiet woman do that to her husband? How could she have wreaked such carnage only to then turn the knife on herself? "Hows" and "whys" that were never fully answered for the public, but I knew. I knew because it was in the depths of my own being.

We both believed we had tamed the beast, only for it to come forth when we least expected it. It was then that I knew that I would have to search for a more permanent solution to my issue. If my mother, who was restrained to such a degree that her control appeared effortless, could not stop the rage inside, then what hope did I have?

My forays into curing my condition started with meditation. Then home remedies and herbs. Then medications. Then alternating the three and creating hybrid concoctions until finally I was filling my days with every measure to keep the anger at bay. Separately or all in combination, I could still feel it — the raging hot anger in my veins. After a few years of futile treatments, I turned to religion, any religion. I did not find satisfaction, only a growing anger and unreasonableness.

One fateful evening, while it was clawing at my stomach, I came across an article about Dr. Cecelia Travestere and her research. She had experimented in musical hypnosis, using musical chords to help animals —and then people— to regulate their emotions. Dr. Travestere recently had promising results treating patients with depression and alleviating hallucinations. I only needed to quell the anger, just enough to keep me going. I wrote to her and volunteered myself as a test subject that night.

Dr. Travestere was quick to contact me. It later came out that various psychiatric associations had panned her work and she would not be able to fully fund her research without unpaid volunteers. I did not care about being paid. I cared about being able to live with this.

Her office was in an all but little forgotten area of the city, surrounded by closed buildings and pop-up clinics. The facility itself was outdated, but clean. It looked to have been a former government office repurposed for this kind of one-on-one work. The bathroom was small and old, a foaming soap dispenser on a beige Formica countertop. The "rooms" were large, larger than necessary and carpeted with that close-knit deep blue carpet that you see in schools or DMVs. All of this was largely comforting, familiar. Dr. Travestere's assistant took my information without any commentary or judgment. I had pictured a sterile facility with white rooms and walls, but instead this could have been an impoverished doctor's office. It oddly set me at ease.

Dr. Cecelia Travestere was just as unassuming. I had also pictured her as some distant researcher, as there had only been one blurry photo of her in the write-up of her research. She was much like the place — neat, if a little out of date. Between the loud pattern on the shirt visible beneath her lab coat, her decidedly oversized and highly unflattering glasses and her light hair pulled into a soft bun at the nape of her neck, I could have guessed any age from thirty to sixty and easily been off by twenty years. She was not cold however, not distant in the slightest. She smiled with an authentic warmth and shook my hand with care.

Her assistant briefed her on my health and medical history and she nodded along. Finally, she turned to me and asked, "So, what is it you want to work on?"

My mouth went dry for a moment. "I don't want to be angry anymore."

Perhaps it was a pallid white in the florescent lights or the dust from the carpet, but for a moment I could have sworn I saw it: Rage flashed in her eyes, and I knew she understood what I had meant.

For the procedure I was told to lie back on a hospital bed in the center of one of the darkened rooms. From its patina, it was easy to guess that this used bed was a discount find. For a few minutes I contemplated this bed, taking in the slight rust and yellowed plastic on it. I wondered how many of her other volunteers had been on this same surface. I wondered how many hospital patients had been on it as well. And I wondered, rather morbidly, how many had died. This thought stirred up my anger and I had to breathe deeply to set it at ease.

What I had read about her research had been lacking on details. All I really knew was that it was non-invasive and involved sound. More accurately, she explained, it involved music. Dr. Travestere had discovered a number of musical chords and rhythms that isolated portions of the brain. Her work involved using subliminal music as a way to soothe or stimulate portions of brain activity. This allowed subjects another avenue to regulate their thoughts and feelings long after they had stopped "listening". My treatment was to come to this facility three times a week and lie down in a darkened room as they played specially prescribed music too low for human hearing. I would be interviewed on my state before and after as a way to track my progress.

It seemed simple enough, harmless and a suspiciously all too easy solution to my problem. The rage sparked for a moment when this crossed my mind, but then I realized I had nothing to lose if it did not work. I lay back and closed my eyes.

If you were to ask me to hum the melody that was played I could not. It does not play in my memory. I only have the faintest notion of what it was, like a bird seen from the corner of your eye as it flies away. Sometimes the click of a door or the strum of a harp or the shuffle of a shoe will seem to trigger a memory of it. But it's only the lightest touch of familiarity, and never feels quite right. I long to hear it, even now, but when I try to remember it, it is as if there is an itch deep in my ear canal that I cannot reach. I try not to think on it too much. At the time there was only me, the "quiet," the hospital bed and the dark.

What I can tell you is that the treatments worked. Even after that first session, I felt a lightness I had never had before. My anger had been subdued, and it only became more acutely obvious as the weeks went by. It was not simply that the monster in me had fallen to sleep; it felt as if it had been removed from my being. It showed in my relaxed demeanor, my languid poses and even on my face. My smile was no longer a futile attempt to conceal an inner tumult — it was authentic joy. My body grew soft, no longer firm in its tension. It was harmonious. It was a miracle.

After a year of this heavenly peace, Dr. Travestere's study ran out of funding. She was to sell her building and was under investigation for unlawful research and at risk of losing her license. I was not moved to anger at this, such was the efficacy of her work. Nor was I even moved to resentment when I read that a colleague of hers had received a grant for a similar study.

In order to continue my treatment, she was kind enough to give me disc with the music that they had been playing for me. I was instructed to limit it to three hours a week and to keep the volume down, just below hearing. She was very adamant that I not turn up the sound for any reason. With this disc in my hand and a promise to follow these instructions to the letter, I embarked on my own self-medication.

This worked, for a time. Life without anger is a peculiar thing, for you become addicted to serenity and shun anything that may disrupt it. I stopped caring for things in my life. My work suffered perhaps, but because I had no intention, ambition or complaints I was promoted at work. I even began to date, but this was unsatisfying for me, although the men did not seem to care one way or another.

After months of the same I felt it again, the little burn in my chest. It came suddenly and without full knowledge of why. All I remember is walking past a building and seeing my reflection in a glass door. There it was—the thing I had tried to keep hidden my entire life, staring back at me with my reflection. I began to panic and increased my treatments. Just an extra hour a week, and then two, and then three. Still, the anger did not stop. It came to pass that I was spending almost all my time listening to the music I could not hear to try and cage that beast. But it would not hold.

Then I broke the promise I had made even further. I raised the volume just a bit. Just enough to hear it, hoping to drown out the sounds of my rage that had made my own skin untenable. Even now I cannot describe it. I remember it was a simple melody, hypnotic. The closest I can come to a description is that it was like delicate feet hitting the stage during a ballet. Rhythmic, drowned out by other noise. It put me at ease for a few blissful hours.

My heartbeat seemed to mimic it and I found myself walking out of my small apartment into the street in a daze. Before I knew it, I had walked miles across the city in the dark into the heat of its nightlife. In the center of town on a busy street was a large, loud nightclub. The neon lights made strange patterns on the concrete and I followed, only to end up on the sidewalk in front of the place. Outside, as within, people where thickly packed together. The smells assaulted me: the alcohol, the cologne and perfumes, the sweat, the exhaust from passing taxis. There were speakers outside, blasting music, drowning out the peace I had found.

I had forgotten the sound that had sedated me, completely and absolutely.

The animal beneath ripped itself free of its chains. I heard nothing and everything from that moment on. Somehow the beat of the P.A. music had merged with sounds of footfalls all around me to create a strange new sound inside my head. Dr. Travestere's prescription music had been replaced in a single moment by something heavy and primal. I knew only the lights, the smells, the sounds, the rage. Everything became impossibly bright and loud for a split second. And then, all at once, it went black and silent.

I do not remember much after that. There were screams,

shouts and music of a rhythm I only partially recognize. There is still blood drying under my fingertips. There is the smell of it on my clothing and the taste on my tongue. Shattered glass is etched into parts of my body. There is a ripped arm, not my own, in my hand and a number of slaughtered bodies left around me. There is a tune I keep humming that I can't seem to get out of my head.

So, what can I tell you of all that? Of all my work to contain my nature? I can tell you that I no longer crave a cage.

SOME DREAMS JUST AREN'T WORTH THE TROUBLE

SHE THINKS ABOUT IT. *WHAT IS THAT WORD? IT MEANS THE same as sweet. Oh yes. Saccharine. Sac-cha-rine. Sac -cah- reen. Lolita? Saccharine. Sweet, sweet, oily sugar. The ceiling, all of it dripping sugar. Mouthwatering, comforting, sticky sweetness. A candyland. The ceiling looked saccharine. That isn't how you are supposed to use the word*, she thinks. *Well, who cares?* No one is with her. Just the eyes of collected dead pigeons and the stuffed animals upon which she is lying. They, of course, would say nothing to contradict her; they would say nothing at all. Unless she was on a really messed up high or worse — then all bets were off.

The ceiling looks saccharine, like it is dripping with candy. She almost opens her mouth, but she resists. Perhaps some-where in her mind she realizes it is not candy but oily water leaking in from the room above in the abandoned and condemned building in which she is squatting. Her name: Emily. Sometimes she forgets it. Emily, sometimes like sugar on the tongue, other times it makes your tongue too full and large. The stuffed animals squirm beneath her in response to her own movements: Some of them are found, some stolen, and not one of them is in pristine condition. A beautiful girl of twenty-eight who still wears blonde hair in pigtails. Her mother used to call her her "little china doll" because of her perfectly smooth face and big expressive eyes.

It smells in this building, but no one else is there to notice the scent of stale piss, shit, mold, and rotting wood. There is also a hint of sweetness to the air due to the sugary scent of decay from the dead rats and mice kicked to the corner. She has propped up the dead pigeons, maggots and all, along the walls so their dead eyes can keep watch over her. Emily lives as an echo in this place and in the world, all messed up, forgotten in her crumbling squatter's castle.

Make no mistake, she is loved and missed, because to her family and friends she has gone missing. Emily just walked out the door one day in a partial cloud of consciousness with a pink bag of belongings (essential and superfluous), and hitchhiked the seven hundred miles to where she is now. Hell, Emily doesn't even know the name of the city she is in, just that it has a lot of pretty parks. At home she is Missing and Presumed Dead.

Today would be a nice day to take a walk, she thinks, when her high begins to come down and her energy comes up a bit. After a nap, Emily will get up, get pretty, and go for a walk. Maybe she will get something to eat. Then come home and get high. A productive day with no crime. She feels too tired and out of it to steal today, and she really doesn't need anything. There will be plenty of food in the dumpster outside the Italian place on the corner. Oh, and the Krispy Kreme doughnuts thrown out at midnight.

Who knows what time it is when Emily wakes up and rolls out of bed. Emily certainly doesn't. She goes to the decrepit shower and gets herself clean. Despite the grotesque conditions she lives in, Emily does her best to stay clean. Cleanliness is next to Godliness after all. She recites that saying over and over again and she bathes in the mildew-ridden basin of rainwater (except the clogged toilet, she shits in a bucket). Emily repeats this saying both vocally and mentally in her mother's voice. *Cleanliness is next to Godliness, Cleanliness is next to Godliness. Cleanliness. Godliness. Clean God. God Clean. Dog Naelc.* Her head starts spinning and she throws up. Emily just keeps on washing, scrubbing hard with her hands until she is as red as a lobster.

After a thorough washing, she pats herself dry with stolen napkins and dirty clothes. Emily prides herself on her forethought to have taken the cluster of napkins: That is to say when she is coherent. She goes to the mirror and brushes her hair precisely one hundred times. *One, two, three, four...* Just like she has been taught. She works for several minutes on her hair part and pulls her hair up into high, tight pigtails with fraying rubber bands. Emily knows they are ready when her scalp turns red. She slathers on some makeup: bright pink eyeshadow and blush. To match she puts on a giant pink monstrosity of a dress — all sequins, tulle, and pink. The dress is one of her favorites: She wore it when she won her third first-place pageant trophy, six years ago. Now it is missing half its sequins and sports torn tulle. Pink. Pink. Pink. *Pink!* All pretty pink. Emily looks in the shards of mirror, still high, now clean and dressed, and thinks: *Beautiful.* Don't forget the lipstick Emily! "Missing and Presumed Dead."

Of course, she is still too bombed to recognize that she looks ridiculous prancing and skipping down the street. Cute on a girl two decades younger, now it's just disturbing. But prance she does before all the gawking strangers. And it only feels better as the pick-me-up she took before she left, just a little, really more of a taste to that cloud nine feeling, starts to kick in.

The stares, well they only validate how beautiful she is. Smiling and waving like a prom queen to anyone who looks her way, she graces the late afternoon streets. Emily, beautiful Emily. She imagines what they must be thinking about her: *Oh, what a pretty young lady, Such a beauty, Well isn't she just a peach, What a ray of sunshine, Must be a princess, Must be a queen!* But you can guess what most everyone is really thinking: "What the...?"

The reality Emily thinks she inhabits is not the reality the rest of us know. To her, the long-exaggerated looks are just the looks of her adoring public. She hums as she approaches the park. This park probably looks better in her mind than it really is, so we'll imagine what she sees: majestic trees bursting with vibrant green leaves rising from soft grass that you could just lie in like a bed. Birds, real birds chirping and singing away in those trees. Beautiful, wonderful, amazing birds. *They sound so pretty and sweet* she thinks. And man, do those flowers smell great! Not a dropped soda can or beer bottle in sight that Emily notices. No, she just prances down the friendly sidewalk like the beauty queen she is.

Up ahead there is a small crowd. Well, that piques Emily's interest. Our little heroine comes up to see that they are watching a street performer. A magician! How quaint, and he is pulling out all the favorites: rabbit from a hat, card tricks, the solid rings that separate, and every other corny and played out gag in the book. But man, the kids are eating it up! So is Emily —she is enchanted by the man in suit, cape and top hat as he gracefully waves his jewel-tipped magic wand. In her eyes he is some weird mesh of a wizard and a knight in shining armor brandishing a sword. Her messed up head believes he is magic, and she is delighted. She can't look away. She cheers and claps at every trick. She holds her breath in before every revelation. She loves his clean-shaven square jaw and perfect smile, she doesn't notice his missing tooth or the large mole on his cheek. This magic is so exciting. Her favorite is when he pulls the dove out of a napkin— it's stuffed, he can't afford to keep a real bird. When he finishes his shtick and packs up, picking up the change in the box, Emily stays. Their eyes meet, and he is in love.

No, not really. This isn't that kind of story.

No, what the Astounding Liam— that's his stage name, not very original— sees is a big doe-eyed mess. But he knows that look and that mess, for he was a heroin addict and homeless two years ago. He got himself arrested and turned his life around. What he sees is a beautiful woman in that drugged up stupor and he thinks: *Hey, I can save her. I can mold her. Shit, she's hot, I may just get laid.* He mistakes this for love, his heart being mostly in the right place, so we can't blame him for approaching her and offering a meal.

"Did you enjoy the show?"

"Oh yes! So much!"

"You can call me The Astounding Liam," he says bowing gallantly, "or just Liam. And you are?"

"I'm Emily."

She puts out her hand and he sees her dirty, chipped nails, but he still kisses it.

"Would you like to grab a bite?"

"Oh! I would love to!"

Liam takes her to a nearby burger place, it's cheap but clean. Emily is curious about these unusual feelings she's having and she thinks she may be in love with this knight, too. She thinks he's got real bona fide magic. She asks all about his tricks, but a magician never reveals his secrets. Liam orders for her and tells her his life story while he continuously glances down at her perfect tits — all thanks to Dr. Wexel, he's a magician in his own right (they were a gift for her eighteenth birthday). He tells her about how he grew up on the wrong side of town... yadda yadda... drugs...needles... Then he gets to the part where he gets arrested and has that wake-up call in jail. Now he has a good job at the grocery store and does magic on his days off 'cause he loves it and it's a little extra cash. Here's the good part: He leans across the table, puts his hand over hers and says "I can help you, you know. I've been where you're at, and I know what you're going through. Let me help you."

Of course, Emily says yes.

Liam takes her home with him, leading our girl gently into his bachelor pad. He gives her a large T-shirt and boxers to change into and tells her that the bathroom is the first door on the right. When she has washed herself again, this time with soap, brushed her hair with the small comb a hundred times *one, two, three, four...*, and folded her favorite dress just the right way she comes out.

He has been waiting on the couch for a long time wondering what had happened. Her tea is getting cold. When she comes out, she notices sadly that he has also changed out of his magician's outfit into some sweat pants and a T-shirt as well. It reads in garish orange letters: "The Fourth Annual Magic Conference." The magic has disappeared. She notices that the bird he pulled out before is lying on the table. She sees its fake glass eyes and grows more chagrined. Emily's high is waning a bit, this is just one of those cohesive cycles, close to withdrawal but not quite. He hands her the cup of microwaved tea and sits her on the couch, trying to decide his next move. Does he turn on the TV? Ask her about herself? No, she may not be comfortable.

He feigns confidence. "Would you like something else?" he asks with his best performer's smile.

"No, I'm fine." Emily's wide eyes curiously scan the room. She is becoming more and more coherent as she sits. It's a lucid cycle, which will go away. She looks to see if there are things she would like to take with her when she leaves. Soap ... yes, this shirt ... yes, maybe some canned food, definitely the bird. He isn't so attractive close up. It's a pretty tidy little place he has.

"So, where do you live?" he said, trying to goad some relevant information from her.

"Oh, a place." Her eyes continue to wander. A book, half wrapped in brown paper on the floor, with a beautiful bird on the cover. She picks it up. *The Learner's Guide to Ornithology.*

"Oh that, my uncle's a big bird watcher and sent me that for my birthday. Do you like birds?" Liam says, trying to catch her eyes and noticing that perfect upturned nose, also thanks to Dr. Wexel. *Damn,* he thinks, *she's really gone. Do I still take her to bed? Nah, won't be good tonight.* "Maybe you should stay here for a while, I can take care of you while you get clean." He lays a hand on her shoulder.

Far away she answers "Okay." Emily will definitely be taking the book when she leaves, and she has stopped listening.

It's getting late. Our knight in shining armor sets her up on the couch with a few old blankets and pillows, and says goodnight. He heads to his room, rubs one out, then lays down for a deep and elated sleep. *I'm going to save her,* is his last thought. In his dreams he plots out their future together: They'll grow close as she gets clean. They'll live together and she'll get a job as a receptionist or something. On his days off she'll act as his beautiful assistant during the show, drawing lots of crowds and coin. They'll fuck like animals. They'll get married, move into a nice house and have some kids. Liam's almost more delusional than Emily. He thinks it's all the drugs, but the drugs are a relatively small problem. The slurred words, hallucinations, and empty eyes are what brought the drugs, not vice-versa. "The doctor doesn't know shit," mama said driving home. Maybe he didn't. Bipolarity, schizophrenia, maybe even borderline psychosis—neither that doctor nor any of the others they'd seen were quite sure. Emily didn't fit in one state just right. She lingers in a world that is sometimes the real one, but often not. Clozapine, Lorazepam, Diazepam, Depakote, Wellbutrin, Invega, and Lithium later, nothing worked quite right. The ones that were close made her tired and gain weight and "We can't have that," as Mama said. She got connected, got on new shit and used that to feel better, taking anything and everything she could buy or steal. One day she thought *Huh, I'm doing all right. I'm going to get out of here,* and Mama convinced her of it later that day when she started yelling. For the past few weeks her routine has been she getting up, getting high, shitting, pissing, eating, stealing, getting high and sleeping; almost like clockwork. It's really been quite peaceful.

All night *The Learner's Guide to Ornithology* keeps her attention. *Ornithology. Or-ni-thaw-li-gee. Ohr-nih-thaw-logy.* It tastes like such a sweet word, and the study so wonderful. Bird after beautiful bird in their nests and in flight. In case you didn't notice by her macabre decor, she loves birds. Mama thought they were filthy, but Emily adored them. Their grace and poise like the perfect pageantry. They were the beauty queens of the natural world. Birds were real-life angels and all that shit. As a little girl, Emily pretended she was a bird, jumped out of a tree, broke her arm and ankles. That moment of flight was the best high she ever had. Emily dreams of birds.

In the morning, Liam finds her drooling on the book. She could do no wrong; he found it endearing. He showers, dresses, has a protein bar and some coffee, then writes a note about where to find the food and his work number. He asks his neighbor to check up on her every once in a while, before he heads to work. The neighbor barely listens, does not care and will do no such thing, even as he nods. Liam has a skip in his step as he walks to the bus. He envisions a glorious future and he can't wait to get home to start it with her.

When Emily wakes up in the afternoon, she reads and tosses the note away like an annoyed kitten given an offensive toy. She eats, showers and brushes her hair a hundred times *one, two, three, four...,* packs up some of his shit and leaves for home. *Take the book and the bird.* She is amazingly coherent for being in withdrawal, a state she will fix soon enough.

Needless to say, Liam is pissed when he gets home. *Can't trust a junkie,* he thinks as he slams through the apartment. "That bitch, that fucking ungrateful fucking bitch!" He calls the police. In some ways, he has dodged a bullet. There was no way he could save her. He isn't a knight in shining armor and he has no magic.

The wind has tilted Emily's birds so she meticulously puts them back. Emily finds her stash and does a nice big dose. She lays back on her bed of stuffed animals enjoying the book. The dove, peacock, and mockingbird race by. No, fly by. The high comes, a peaceful, wonderful, exciting high. Better than any orgasm. The hallucination comes too (chemical or biological, you decide). Birds, their wings flap. *Emily, mmm ih lee,* the call, the sound of a wing cutting the air. The hum of the humming bird. *MMMM, ihhhh leee. What bird is Emily? Emilia Aves, sounds nice. Or is it Aves Emilia? Aves Emily. A-vez-Ehm-ih-le. Chirp, chirp. Whistle. MMM. I can fly. Mama, I'm gonna fly. Fluh-I.*

Before long, Emily takes some of her precious collection and excitingly sets about ripping the wings off the bird carcasses. Sometimes she uses shards of broken mirrors to help

out, cutting her hands without noticing. She peels off her clothing. *Need something sticky. Shit, use shit.* She slathers it on her
back, and painfully poses the wings along her spine. Picture it,
a beautiful girl of twenty-eight, naked, with tight perfect
pigtails. Her back is covered with globs of old shit with ripped
off decaying pigeon wings perched in them, some of which are
sliding off. This beautiful girl in a rundown, broken building.
It's a sight. Picture it, her ass, her back, her perfect tits, perfect
nose and a wildly excited gleam in her eyes. That bright smile.
Picture it now. Emily runs up to the roof, four stories high,
barely needing to catch her breath. The sun is high like her,
and the wind is working right. She gets a running start, closes
her eyes, smiles, and leaps off...

Let's pretend she really did it.

LA BRUJA Y EL VENDEDOR OR HOW EDUARDO FOUND HIS HEART

Author's note: This story is written, for lack of a better phrase, in Spanglish. I grew up in a bilingual household, and stories were never a 100% English, or 100% Spanish. To honor this and to honor where my mother comes from, Chile, I wrote this story. I hope you enjoy it.

ONCE UPON A TIME THERE WAS A TRAVELING SALESMAN who was named Eduardo. Eduardo sold hats, -*los sombreros más lindos del mundo. Sombreros para los padres, niños, rancheros y sacerdotes.*[1]- He would chant while bouncing into the village. The children would come and stare at Eduardo, for he carried every hat he sold on his back and on his head. It was quite a sight!

All the women would come when he arrived at the village as well, for Eduardo was very handsome. Even though he carried all those hats, caminó como un príncipe. He had a voice like the easy roll of thunder y una sonrisa that shone like light breaking through a cloud. He traveled from village to village in the valley of a mountain range and wherever he went, the young women would smile and flirt with him. They all wanted to marry him and the young womens' mothers wanted him to marry their daughters. -*¿Y cuando te vas a casar Eduardo?* -una Señora would ask, indicating her daughter with the tilt of her chin or a batted eyelash.

Eduardo would just laugh that booming laugh of his, -*cuando me enamore* - would be his answer, and he would soon move on to another village. It came to pass that while Eduardo found many women beautiful and charming, he did not feel he could love them. Even Serena Del Río, the most beautiful woman in all the villages, with her dark hair and skin as clear as still water, could not move his heart to love.

On a hot summer day, after turning down Serena's hand, Eduardo sat down at the foot of a mountain with all his hats and seriously considered this. He found many women pretty and he often felt something for them, but he had never fallen in love, or at least he could never tell if he had. While Eduardo was thinking, one of the respected men of the village, Don Juan Carlos, came to see him in his pensive state. -*¿Qué te pasa amiguito?* - asked Don Juan Carlos, -*¿Por qué tienes esa cara?*

Don Juan Carlos was a respected ranchero with a lovely wife and many good children, and people often looked to him for his wisdom. Eduardo told him everything, about how he did not feel his heart stir for any woman beyond simple physical attraction. Eduardo confided in Don Juan Carlos that he feared he would never fall in love and have a beautiful wife to come home to, or a woman to bear his children and fix his meals.

After hearing this, Don Juan Carlos stroked his chin as he thought. Then caramba! Se la prendió el bombillo, Don Juan Carlos seemed to have solved the problem. He looked at Eduardo with a face as serious as stone - *¡Amiguito, creo que no* *es un problema tuyo solamente! La bruja que vive arriba de la Montaña te ha hechado una maldicion y te robo tu corazón!*

This is how Eduardo heard of the witch who steals the hearts of young men, and he resolved then to find and confront her. Con todos sus sombreros, Eduardo made his way up the mountain. This was no quick and easy trek, even for one as young and strong as Eduardo. The air was thinner and cold. The terrain was hard to climb, for the soil was shallow in many places and his boots could not grasp it. At night he would build himself a little shelter from his many sombreros and brew mate tea to ease the pain all over his body. But Eduardo was determined to get his heart back from the witch and one day fall in love.

He reached the witch's cottage early one morning. It was built on the slope of the mountain and he could see a small garden y un corral con cabras y alpacas. Eduardo put his large stack of hats aside, straightened his back and knocked on the door. The woman who answered Eduardo no era la mas linda del mundo, no linda como Serena Del Río, pero de una manera muy peculiar era linda. Eduardo was shocked, for he thought that a witch who lived on a mountain would be an old crone, not this young woman with a delicate face, high cheeks y ojos claros.

Eduardo blinked himself back to reality and looked the witch straight in her bright eyes. In his booming voice he said - *¡Bruja! ¡Tu te robaste mi corazón! ¡Da me lo que me robaste!*

La bruja looked at Eduardo quizzically. Who was this stranger who had come to her solitary home to accuse her of stealing his heart? She looked at the handsome salesman, whom she realized would have been even more attractive had he not just spent several days struggling up the mountain, and replied *-Yo no le robe su corazón pero lo tomaré si me lo da.*

With that, the witch went around her little farm to do her

daily work. She milked the goats, fed and brushed the alpacas, dug for potatoes and planted more. Eduardo watched, confused. What did she mean she would take his heart if he gave it? He settled in to stay for a while, hoping that perhaps she would accidentally drop his heart somewhere and he could take it back. He built a little shelter out of his sombreros and observed her as she worked around her casita.

That evening, she left her casita and approached Eduardo's shelter con un vaso de té. She had seen him out there in the cold and taken pity on him. In the moonlight, she looked even more beautiful. Her skin seemed to glow and her dark hair faded into the starry sky like it was made con el cielo. Eduardo felt something stir in his chest.

Pero eso no es amor.

It was attraction. Eduardo had felt that for many beautiful women, but he knew it was a fleeting feeling. A feeling easily replaced con una nueva cara linda. This witch looked at Eduardo's little setup and invited him to her fire for tea y sopa. At this Eduardo felt something else stir in his chest.

Pero eso no es amor.

That was kindness. Kindness was something he had given and received on his many travels around the valley. He was thankful every time. Part of him still feared this was a witch's trap, but he was so cold, hungry and tired that he could not say no. They ate in silence. The small meal filled his belly and he slept, warm and silent, in front of her fire. Esa noche Eduardo soño de su corazón y de una mujer con ojos claros.

The next morning, the witch woke up with the dawn and worked around her casita. Eduardo watched her move, admiring her grace and extreme efficiency. He noted how clever she was, having rigged up a device that collected eggs and another that snared small creatures. He again felt that little stirring in his chest.

Pero eso no es amor.

That was admiration. Eduardo knew that feeling, of seeing something accomplished or done that you hoped to aspire to. Watching how the witch moved in the difficult climate with such ease, coming up with ways to survive, Eduardo was impressed.

He figured that since he was there, and she was sharing her hardly sparse meals with him, he should help. He combed and sheared her alpacas for her. As a man who knew fabric from his trade, he had never seen fur so fine and soft. He brought the fur to her and watched as she shaped it into wool, her hands and fingers moving la lana con una destreza que solo una bruja pudiese tener.

He asked if her skill was because of her witchcraft and she just laughed. The warmness of her laugh made something stir in Eduardo's chest.

Pero eso no es amor.

That was just camaraderie. He liked to hear her laugh, and yearned to make her laugh again. When she finished, she explained that no, ella no era una bruja. Y que los campesinos de alrededor no concevían come una mujer le gustava vivir sola y por eso llamaban "Bruja".

-Bueno, yo no voy a llamarte 'bruja' entonce. ¿Como te llamas? - Pregunto Eduardo.

-Me llamo Marta. -she said, con una sonrisa.

Paso el año y Eduardo and Marta were no longer living apart. He moved into her casita and they lived together on that mountain. Eduardo incorporated Marta's wool into the hats he sold. He smiled more than before, but he no longer had wandering eyes for the maidens of the different villages. After every trip to the valley to sell sombreros, Eduardo would find himself eager to come back to Marta. Often, when he was around her, he felt that little stirring in his chest. Sometimes she would look at him and he would know that she felt it too. They always felt better together.

The years went by and Eduardo was no longer the young, handsome gentleman before who had determinedly scaled that mountain. His back was bent from carrying su sombreros y su pelo estaba gris. La cara de Marta estaba arrugada, su cabello lucia como el color del cielo por la noche y con una nubesita blanca. Yet, despite being old and frail, their hearts still fluttered around each other.

Porque éso si es amor.

Love was not one singular feeling for Eduardo and Marta, it was the combination of all these wonderful feelings they had for one another. It was the closeness and necessity of togetherness and companionship that did not falter, but grew with age.

Y ellos vivieron felices para siempre.

MUTATIO

THE SWAMP KING

ONCE THERE WAS AN OLD, RICKETY HOUSE BETWEEN A large orange grove and an ancient, hidden swamp. It was a small cottage perched on stilts to account for the times the nearby river flooded. It always seemed a little unsteady. If a hard storm came, the walls would creak, and the house would sway this way and that. The people who lived inside could live and die by the strength of the storm, always fearing that a harsh one would blow them over.[1]

This cottage sat next to the orange grove, so when the wind blew west the air would smell like sweet fresh citrus. But when the wind blew east, it would be the hot moss-ridden breeze of untamed wet air and decay. The swamp had a fierce reputation for the people who lived near it. It was filled with poisonous snakes, alligators, and predators of all kinds. If the rain came, there was no safety from the climbing waters. More than one hunter had disappeared in that swamp looking for game, and search parties were often too afraid to search inside. They said that in that swamp was a cursed king, who reigned over the wilderness and kept people at bay. It was said that this Swamp

King traded in the fearsome and unruly magic which was endemic to the swamp.

In that rotting little cottage lived Silvia and her stepfather. While most fathers love their daughters, and most daughters love them back, Silvia and her stepfather carried no such affection. Silvia's father was as cruel to her as he had been to her mother when she was alive. When Silvia's mother dared to try to leave, promising Silvia that she would come back to her, she was found frozen by a mysterious spell a mile away from the cottage. In her worst nightmares, Silvia still remembered her mother's horrified face behind that strange block of ice that refused to melt in the heat of summer. Silvia desperately wanted to escape herself too, but she feared she'd be frozen as well, or worse. That fear kept her imprisoned by her stepfather, frightened of the beasts and wild magic that lay in wait.

That's how it remained until the day that fear of the unknown beyond the cottage was no longer enough to keep her chained to lingering gaze of her stepfather. In the years since her mother had passed, Silvia had grown into a beautiful young woman. She had delicate long limbs like the roots of a mangrove and lips as red as a scarlet snake's collar. Her dark hair trailed behind her like the branches of a willow as she swept and did the cleaning. Silvia had a habit of sneaking off and climbing up the orange trees like a spider to gorge herself on the fresh sweet fruit. One day, with the juice of the fruit on her chin, while the wind blew east, Silvia's step-father grabbed her wrist, looked her in the eye and said "You know, you look a lot like your mother when we met."

That night during the large, low-hanging full moon, Silvia decided that she needed to get away. Despite the overwhelming threat of rogue curses or fearsome creatures, she crept out of the cottage and gazed at the shadowed lands. If she went east into the orange grove, she could easily end up caught by her wicked stepfather. In the west, the swamp's moonlit pine trees beckoned. Those branches seemed to call to her as they swayed in the warm night.

Silvia set out into that vast swamp, less afraid of the poisonous critters than of the shadow of her stepfather. She walked for miles, avoiding snakes and dangerous pitfalls. Every few steps she heard a new and more frightening noise, like the lingering hoot of an owl or call of a turkey vulture. Vines hung down in the hammocks, seemingly clawing at her in the dark. She waded in the shallow waters, sawgrass cutting at her suntanned skin, making a million little incisions. Mosquito-bitten and exhausted, she stopped in the early morning light at the cradle of a cypress tree and, nestling herself there, fitfully fell asleep.

When she awoke it was to a low sound like that of a bull-frog. But it was not a harmless amphibian. Instead, staring at her from a few feet out across the water, was the largest gator Silvia had ever seen. She looked around as the creature swam closer and closer, its tail undulations sending ripples to the shore of the small lake. Silvia wanted to get up, she wanted to run but something in the gaze of that gator kept her fixed in place. The knees of the cypress, which last night cocooned her in a comforting embrace, had become a prison. The gator made its way to shore and climbed up to the nook where Silvia cowered. He opened his massive jaws, jaws that could swallow Silvia whole and said...

"What are you doing in my kingdom, girl?" The gator's voice was a deep croak.

"I was running away from my stepfather, who wants me to take my mother's place," Silvia replied, suddenly regretting her decision to run.

"And so you ran into the swamp, where my subjects can eat you up and use your bones like toothpicks." When the gator closed its maw, she could see he had human-looking eyes—blue irises surrounded by milky white corneas—and that along the top of his head were jagged lumps of scar tissue that looked like a rough crown. She had thought the tale of the Swamp King a fantasy, but now here she was, face to face with that very legend.

"I had nowhere else to go. Are you going to eat me?"

"You've entered my home during a full moon, uninvited. Our laws are clear that you are fair game. How lucky for you that I am a kind king and have just eaten."

Only then did his uninvited guest notice that several anhinga feathers were stuck in the alligator's teeth.

"Thank you, your highness," Silvia said, forcing herself out of a momentary daze. "How do I repay this kindness?"

"A human wishes to grant me a favor then?"

"Yes," she said, not knowing what exactly she could do for the king.

"What is your deepest wish?"

Silvia did not even need to think. "I want my father gone."

The alligator thought silently for a moment. He slammed his tail one, two, three times and two small ibises came to chirp in his ear. The ibises bowed low to the Swamp King and flew off. He thought a moment longer, reading something invisible in Silvia and said, "I can give you my skin to use, to destroy your father, if you would grant me a favor."

Silvia took a second to consider the Swamp King's proposal. She wanted to be free of her stepfather, but she was wary of the kind of bargain a fearsome Swamp King would offer. In the end, nothing seemed worse than the possibility of being caught and dragged home to that evil man. "What is the favor?"

"That will happen after I give you my end of the bargain."

Silvia took the risk with a nod of her head.

The Swamp King let out a roar that shook the very ground

and shed his skin. The Swamp King's skin became a large greenish and brown spotted coat. In his place was an old man, with a white beard that fell to the ground, boney knees wobbling as he stood up. He had an ancient, rusted crown atop his head and he sat down in the crux of the cypress after handing over his skin. The Swamp King looked up at her and said, "To use my skin, you must put it on after the moon comes up. And you must return to me before the light comes. If you do not return in time, the swamp will make its displeasure known."

Silvia agreed, and turned and marched back east to the little cottage. It was sunset when she reached her home. Her father was nowhere to be seen, so she hid behind a ripe orange tree and waited. When the sun finally set and the large moon climbed over the treetops Silvia shouldered the coat. For a moment nothing seemed to be happening, but in the next Silvia sensed a great tingling all over her body. She looked down at her hands to see that she no longer had them but lethal-looking claws instead.

She went into the cabin to find it empty. Her massive footsteps made the stilts of the cottage creak under the pressure. Looking into the mirror she did not see the gator she expected, but something beastly in-between. She had the skin, maw, and tail of a gator, but the stature of a great black bear and the claws of a panther. Silvia had become a grand, powerful monster and she no longer feared seeing her stepfather.

Silvia's stepfather came home well past the stroke of midnight. In the dark, Silvia could see his form by the light of the moon. He seemed smaller than she remembered, and for a moment she almost felt pity. But she recalled how he had dragged her away, screaming, begging and crying, from the frozen corpse of her mother.

She swung her massive tail, hitting the lecher straight in the stomach and knocking him over before his eyes had even adjusted to the darkness. He screamed and tried to hit Silvia the beast with his fist, but she was too fast and slashed off his hand with a single swipe of a claw. She saw the fear in his eyes, and the beast in her smiled a crocodile's smile. Silvia wasted no time chomping him in half and tearing him apart. She dragged what was left of his body to the orange grove and buried it beneath a fallow tree.

But it was getting light and Silvia remembered her promise to the Swamp King. She ran, fearing she would be too late. As her heart quickened, a feeling of incredible lightness came upon her, and she slowly realized that she was no longer running but flying. The Swamp King's coat had turned her into a grand heron and she made it to the King just moments before sunrise.

She hesitated before removing and returning the coat, wishing to keep it. She had never felt such power, or safety, as she had in the disguise. It allowed her to be what she needed to be — what she wanted to be. The Swamp King took the feathered coat in his crooked hand and looked up at Silvia.

"Are you ready to make up your end of the bargain?"

She looked at the old man, whose limbs twisted and creaked, and she nodded.

"You must break this spell that keeps me here. I have been the ruler of this swamp for three hundred years, and now I am old and tired and no longer wish to be king. I hope to rest here forever. But you must willingly take that burden and that power."

Silvia looked at this frail old man, whose flesh had grizzled from age. She thought about how she might never see another person again, forever tied to a swamp. But she also remembered the freedom she felt in flight, and the power she'd felt in her monstrous form. Her decision was clear. Silvia held out her hand and the old King handed her his crown. In her hands, it became a wreath of orchids. With that, Silvia became the Queen of the Swamp.

In time, that little cottage by the orange grove was overrun with ivy and disappeared into the nature surrounding it. Now the swamp has a new reputation. When the wind blows east, it carries with it the scents of magnolia and jasmine. They say that the Swamp Queen is loved and respected by all the swamp creatures, from the tiniest gnat to the spoonbill to the panther. Even the humans nearby look upon that swamp differently. They say that the pure of heart, if they are brave, can cross the swamp in peace. If they are in trouble, they can even ask the Swamp Queen for a favor. But villains who trespass may find themselves between the jaws of a gator.

CHANGE

THE DAY IT HAD BEEN CONFIRMED, SEVEN YEARS PRIOR, Flor's mother Ilda had smiled and clapped. That night, Ilda had cried herself to sleep. Few families had the honor of even one vessel in the line, but Flor's line had been blessed with two others. It was something Ilda had celebrated in their ancestry until it came time to recognize her daughter as one. All the stories of their ancestors, especially the auspicious ones, disappeared when the mark revealed itself on Flor's lower back.

Such was how the mothers of the vessels past had often faced this hurdle. They celebrated it in public and mourned in private. Ilda, no matter how hard she tried, could not keep her grief hidden from Flor. This unnerved Flor, who should have spent her final years as a mortal celebrating her life, instead she had wound up torn between her mother's pain and her own. Flor could feel *it*, underneath, biding its time, waiting to be released. She scratched herself absentmindedly, at the skin holding the being back. She wanted to meet it, to know it, to destroy the goddess inside. But she feared the loss of herself, not to mention the release ceremony itself.

In the time before there had been the Jel, who lived in Valley of the Seven Rivers, and they worshiped many gods. The Jel did not live peacefully or turbulently, they lived rather ordinary lives. Then came the Hickt, who had wanted for much. They had wanted land, power, pain, riches. The Hickt brought a few other nations with them: the Sligyl, the Fatori, and the Entune. They subjugated the Jel and set up a complex hierarchy. They tried to remove the old gods and give forth the new. Little did they know that the gods would talk with each other, and that they would come to an agreement.

As time went on, those hierarchies degraded. The Jel, Hickt, Sligyl, Fatori and Entune melded, aided by a goddess who would appear every hundred years. The goddesses were from the many different cultures, each inhabiting the body of a girl until she could be released to reign. Some years it was a goddess with a penchant for fertility, and the calves would fatten, the crops would flower and the population would soar. Other years it would be a goddess who enjoyed conflict, and there would be blood and chaos. Sometimes it was a goddess who fancied the arts, and she who would usher in an era of enlightenment and innovation. There were many goddesses above and in-between.

The Melyn, or "Free People" as they called themselves, born out of bloody, complex histories, moved closer to peaceable society. For this they praised the goddesses that did come, even the turbulent ones. The goddesses marked their hosts with a silver trail of dots along the back. They needed to be known before bursting forth from the bodies of their vessels.

Flor did not feel anything when the marks first appeared. She had been swimming with friends in a creek tucked away in the trees. As she climbed out of the water, a friend screamed.

What the Melyn did not realize was that benevolence is a fixed characteristic. Some goddesses were kind because it was in their nature to be kind. Others were cruel by design. Once a goddess had chosen a vessel there was no amount of adulation that would modify them. If they came to be kind, they would be kind. If they came to be cruel, that was but the nature of things.

Flor spent much of her youth in silent skepticism. She did not believe that a goddess was inside, incubating until her time to come forward. It was a few months before her seventeenth birthday, before the ceremony that would set her free, when she finally began to feel it. The first sign was subtle— burning, tingling sensation in her hands that she could have easily excused as something else. Next came spasms of pain, extending from navel to groin—sharp, sporadic—pain that grew more acute as time passed.

One night, her eyes burned as if she had a fever, but she had no fever. She awoke the next morning with new eyes: eyes, she realized, that let her see things that others could not. At first, she thought these visions were tricks of the light. Strange shadows made by moving branches or the wings of an insect that had streaked off too fast to see. As the days went on and the images cleared and took shape, she witnessed what appeared to be her grandmother walking through their home. The image could have been solid, the woman's long elegant fingers carrying a bowl of soup to a young child. Flor had never met her grandmother, who had passed years before her birth. She had only seen this woman in pictures, and this image in front of her was younger than that. That was when Flor realized that she was able to see the past.

As the days continued, she would see more images; of buildings that were solid to the touch in disarray; of people with strange faces and thrillingly unfamiliar technology; images of older faces imposed on the living people that were actually physically there before her. That was when Flor realized that she was also seeing the future, and that she was seeing past, present and future all overlapping and playing out before her strange new eyes.

Finally came the voice. One night, only a few moons before the ceremony, as Flor laid curled up in her bed, her head aching from the all the stimulus she had been bombarded with, she heard it as barely a whisper.

"Skilarus," it said.

Flor had never heard that word before, but she knew what it was. It was the language of the gods. Other chosen had mentioned it in their diaries and writing, but none could describe it or translate it. That did not matter. Flor knew it as surely as she knew how to laugh or cry. It was natural, she was a part of it. And she knew she could understand it. She could speak it to the voice if needed.

Skilarus, was a simple salutation: It meant, "I am here."

Two nights later, Flor tested the waters, curled up in her bed.

"[Hello?]" she said, in a tongue that was foreign but close to breathing.

"Skilarus. [We are together. It is good to be almost whole,]" it said.

"[We? Are there more of you?]" Flor replied

"[No. Just you and I. Soon we will not be separate. We will be one again as we were before.]"

Flor dug deeper into her covers. "[What do you mean?]"

"[You and I are the same. We are incomplete until united. Until we are *one.*]" The voice paused and Flor knew that it was assessing something about itself. "[Are we in pain?]"

"[Sometimes. The headaches are the worst, but they are getting better. Why do you care?]"

"[There is no 'me and you,' only us. Only an incomplete me.]" Another pause. The voice was measuring something in itself. Flor could feel it. "[I am in pain.]" It paused again. "[I have been in pain for years now. Since I put myself into this vessel.]"

Flor could feel it, the pain, the longing. She could feel the missing, bleeding, raw portions of herself elsewhere. Calling to her. Imploring her to join them. She closed her eyes and took a deep breath, a breath that was not hers. She could taste something: earthy, smoky. "[Who are you?]"

"[We. We are the coming of things. We are the promise of new.]"

Flor did not speak to the voice in public in much the same reason she did not discuss her pain. Her position as the soon to be goddess was too important to be caught up in human matters. Instead her study of what was to come became more constant the closer as the fateful moment approached. Flor dug herself into the studies of past goddesses and their vessels, sneaking off at all hours to read those histories.

In all the ceremonies, in all the texts, in every gently passed over sentence, she knew why the people in her life pulled themselves away from her. It was a thing better left unsaid, that in order for the goddess to live, she would die. Despite the reassurances the voice whispered to her every night, of joining, of reunification, Flor remained skeptical.

Flor could not escape her fate, but she spent plenty of time contemplating doing just that anyway. If she ran and did not do the ceremony, this goddess clawing her way through her body would kill her. She would also be a shameful memory for her mother and her people. If she did the ceremony she surely would die. As she contemplated the end of her own mortality, Flor found herself pulling away from everyone as well. Or, well —or at least she tried.

Ilda did not treat her daughter like the goddess she would become. She treated her like the child she still believed her to be as much as possible. She scolded her, held her, bossed her around their humble home. Ilda held onto her child as long as she could.

One night, Ilda snuck into her daughter's quarters long after she had fallen asleep. She set a chair beside Flor's bed, sat down quietly and just stared at the sleeping almost-seventeen-year-old. Flor had a chipped, bitten nail on her thumb, telltale evidence of a habit that she could not seem to get rid of, goddess inside or not. When Flor slept this soundly, it reminded Ilda of when her child was a toddler and would fall asleep in her arms in the middle of a family gathering. There could be noise all around, but an infant Flor had found peace in her mother's arms.

Ilda sang softly to herself and her child, stroking Flor's hair. It was a lullaby the Melyn sang to their new babes. The song came from a Jel poem that had been translated and put to music by the Hickt. Mothers often sang it to their children in the many tongues of their people.

"*Let the babe hear sweet songs,*
In the cool dark night,
For my love for you child,
Could blind the stars in the sky."

In the middle of her song Flor's eyes opened. But the eyes that shone through were not her daughter's. Ilda paused. She knew these eyes as well.

Flor, but not Flor, sat up and looked Ilda directly in the eye. "Thank you," she said in an accent more ancient than the stone beneath their feet. "Thank you for having kept your part of the bargain."

Ilda looked away at a corner where Flor, still a young mortal, had left her vestments in a pile. "Do you have to take her from me? Truly? Can you not simply leave it as it was?"

"We are what we were always. You knew this." The being inside Flor rubbed her own shoulders, brushing away a chill.

"She will be here, for I am here. She is me, my spirit made flesh. This was the deal we made."

"I thought... I thought it would be different. I was desperate and did not know what I was doing when I made that deal."

Flor, but not Flor, picked at that chipped nail. She tucked a knee beneath her and looked at Ilda.

"When last we met, the child in your womb had ceased to live. You begged for one of my kind to save her. I gave you myself, and asked only that you raise me as your daughter."

"I remember the dream. I did... I did not know what I was doing. My husband was ill and I did not know if we would be able to make another. This was my fourth, I couldn't bear it if-if, I... I thought it would be fine. But losing her... I..." Ilda coughed and heaved.

"It has always been this way between our kind. That you misunderstand our nature is typical. Flor is not only your daughter. She is me, the me that needed to learn from your people. She is the portion that I made and tore off myself. Now I will be complete and able to walk among you."

"But why, but why me?" Ilda truly wanted to say "her."

"Because the stars aligned for us that day. Because I needed a mother. Because you asked." The Flor that was not Flor looked Ilda directly in the eyes, meeting a gaze that she had seen every day these past seventeen years. Ilda felt her ache.

"If it will help, know that our pain at the joining does not last." Flor that was not Flor pushed a strand of hair behind her ear.

Ilda wiped at her eyes with her palms. She gulped and heaved a bit more.

The Flor that was not Flor sniffed and wiped her eyes. "Mom?" she said, in a smaller voice than before. "Can you hold me for a little while and sing to me like you used to?"

Ilda had to laugh a bit and wiped her eyes, swallowing her

pain once more. She moved onto the bed and held her child-bound-up-with-a-goddess and stroked her hair. She continued her song.

"Let the babe sleep deeply,
When the nightbird sings,
For my love for you child,
Could melt anything."

In times past, the days leading up to the ceremony meant a number of parties, celebrations, ceremonies and processions. Flor opted for only one small ceremonial celebration and a procession— the absolute minimum. In times past, people would observe the girl vessel to get a sense of what kind of goddess would soon be among them. They would make predictions based on what sorts of ceremonies they would choose and other factors. They would observe the girls with keen eyes for their manners, language, and choice of clothing.

Flor gave nothing away. To everyone's frustration she accelerated the process of detachment she had begun when her Goddess marks had been confirmed. She cut her relations to loved ones and her friends in a hundred little ways. Flor also tried to separate herself from her mother more and more. Ilda gave her space but she refused to be discarded.

To pass the time away from other people, Flor would climb onto a hillside and sit alone watching her city through eyes that saw the passage of time converge. But she was never truly alone, not with the voice becoming more agitated as the days grew close to their "reunification" as it called it. At times it was soothing; not nervous and excitable. Other times it was impatient. But it managed at least one aspect of consistency, in that it steadfastly gave nothing away as to its nature.

Flor found herself lashing out at the voice for this reason. She was melancholy about her impending death and also anxious about what it would entail. And how could she even know what she would become without any clue as to the true nature of the goddess inside? It would coo about the time coming, or how their kind did not assign the same markers humans did. There were no goddesses of things, it explained—of wars, or love, or of art. They simply were.

Three days before the ceremony, as Flor was in one such frustrating, probing, evasive discussion, Ilda came to the hillside. She sat down silently beside her daughter. Flor looked over to this woman who had birthed and raised her, and whom she was attempting to make into a stranger, and took stock of her. She saw the Ilda of the past, young and skinny and graceless; the Ilda that followed—a young mother, far more self-assured; and on to the present, and future, in both of which Ilda looked every bit the woman in mourning, her Jel features strained and elongated in the absence of her family.

Ilda smiled and stroked Flor's hair. "I need to speak to my daughter, if you don't mind."

Flor could feel the voice withdraw, retreating and growing silent for the first time in memory. "But how did you-"

"Before you begin, I need to tell you something. I need to tell you this before it festers in my heart and kills me slowly." Ilda looked out on the city. In this light, golden in the late midday, Ilda's brown skin mimicked the sunset. She continued, "I made a deal—a bargain, a long time ago and it is why you are the way you are. When I was younger, the world seemed full of possibilities, but when I got older and married those possibilities dried up. I loved your father, more than the river loves to run, more that I knew I could love."

Flor recalled the images of her father around their home, the recent visions she had seen with her new eyes. They shared a nose and eyes that had thinner lids. He had died while she was still a baby, and Flor had thus been too young to know anything of him. She knew stories about him, and to her he seemed to be a mythical figure, a ghost in her home, measured by an absence of presence.

"But in those days, I had no real wealth," Ilda said. "My parents used it all in the hard times. A few years before your birth, a sickness came to the city."

Flor remembered hearing about the sun sickness, as it was called. The disease caused people to grow exhausted when they went out during the day. Some recovered, but many others passed away. Others were sick for long periods of time, shuffling to a gradual death.

"Your father and I both had the illness, and because neither of us could work in the fields he went to the city and worked twice as hard to provide for us. I recovered eventually, but he never really did. Your father could do little and I knew I would lose him sooner than I cared. I wanted to keep a part of him alive. I wanted— needed — to keep a part of him with me. We tried very hard for a child as your father grew weaker.

"There were three before you. Two were miscarriages. Another was a stillbirth. I became pregnant with you, but by then your father could barely walk on his own. I prayed to every goddess that ever was. One night, when you weren't kicking, I went to sleep and I had a dream.

"In that dream I met you. Or the goddess you were, the one now inside you. And it offered me a deal: That I might let her save the child inside, that it would be chosen and I would no longer feel the pain of this disease. For you see, my dove, your silence had been a sign that your heart had stopped beating.

"I knew, I knew what it meant." Ilda paused to look at her hands, remembering the hands that shook on this deal. "I knew that I would be sacrificing you for everyone else in seventeen years. I knew that you would have to go through the ceremony or be consumed by it. But I was in a dream, and I was not sure what was real, and your father was dying, and I could not bear to have another dead child in my arms. In my selfishness, I agreed to it."

Ilda took a deep breath, making the tears pause their descent down her face. Flor looked away. She was angry that she would go through all of this for her mother's desperation. In the city, a child was eating a sweet sitting on a corner. She could see that child as she was then, and how she would be as an adult, searching for a shop that had closed. It occurred to her that if it had not been her mother, it would have been some other desperate person.

The voice perked up. "I needed someone to let me in. We cannot make the bond unless a host is willing. This was my first time, and our mother, she was hardened but kind. I wanted to have a life like this. We needed this life and she gave it."

Flor looked at her mother. She gained much from her choice. The mother of a goddess is given food, shelter. The vessel of a goddess is given fine clothes and education. Yet, they could not help but suffer from the choice she had made. Flor could make that suffering less. She took her mother in her arms. They held each other in silence.

The day before the ceremony, the voice went contemplatively silent. Flor refused any last celebrations and rituals. Instead, she ate home cooked meals and wandered around the city. Her special vision relented for a day, if only to give her a few last hours of normalcy. Her city had changed even in her short lifetime. There was the amphitheater, which had had to be expanded for greater crowds. The taller buildings made possible by carrier boxes and pulleys that allowed people to move upwards without climbing. The little school she had attended as a child was now a series of shops with housing above. All things must make themselves anew, or cease to be. Noticing and documenting these changes in her mind was a balm to Flor. Her change was imminent.

On her last night she watched the sunset with Ilda on the hillside. They watched as their city was cloaked in gold and oranges, which faded to a rich blue, and finally black speckled with the glow of lanterns. Flor kept her eyes open the entire time, despite the tears. She wanted to commit every moment to her final memory.

The morning of the ceremony was filled with a desperate quiet. Flor walked with her mother to the shack in the early morning mist. Flor had known about what was to come since she had first been confirmed. She had read the passages about the ceremony over and over, each described it with an intense dedication to medical detail. Reading each step over and over to prepare herself, to steel her nerves for her imminent death, did not in fact steel her nerves. She still shivered when she opened the shack door.

The shack itself was supposed to convey humility, but each decade it had become grander and finer as generations found themselves having to rebuild it when the wooden structure rotted. Inside, Flor was met with the five priestesses who would assist in the transition. She knew their names and faces from over the years even though they had all quite obviously kept their distance from her. Having been trained since youth to perform this act, they did not want to become attached to the sacrificial calf.

Three of the priestesses were pointers, one was a hearth maiden, and the oldest was to be the cleaver. The hearth maiden commenced her task, lighting the fire and throwing in specific herbs to scent the shack. The pointers disrobed and bathed Flor, dusting her with perfumes and oils. They braided and cut her hair, to be set aside and revered at the temple by future generations. They shaved her head for a cleaner incision.

The cleaver sharpened and blessed her knives at the altar. All vessels were given the option to select or design their

knives. In the privacy of their temples the priests and priestesses would speculate about what the choice indicated about
the goddess. The prevailing theory being that if it was a
returning goddess, the vessel would select the same knives as
before.

Flor had chosen a very old, very simple handle design and
only asked that the blades be replaced with the newest,
sharpest material. The priests and priestesses did not know
what to make of this choice. The knives glimmered in the fire-
light, reflecting the shadows that moved across the walls. Flor
closed her eyes.

The pointers tied their ropes around her limbs and waist.
They took their positions at opposite ends of the hut and on the
cleaver's benediction, they used a series of pulleys to hoist her
up, arms and legs splayed, directly over the roaring fire. The
heat caused Flor to sweat, perfumed drops falling and turning
to steam below. Flor kept her eyes closed, sure that she would
die before the hardest part even finished.

The night before, as Flor had lain in her bed trying not to
sleep, she had asked the voice a simple question: "Will it hurt?"

The voice had waited, she could feel it waiting. It finally
answered, "Yes."

"Why? Why do we do this?" Flor had cried into her pillow.

"Until we no longer have to," was all the voice would say.

The hearth maiden heated the knives as the cleaver
climbed a small set of steps to lean over Flor's backside. The
hearth maiden passed a hexagonal knife to the cleaver. The
cleaver took this knife and at the base of her spine, where a
goddess mark had first appeared as a solitary dot, she pierced.
Flor did not scream. She sucked in her breath as the knife
moved above the spine. The cleaver gave it back to the hearth
maiden to be reheated. The hearth maiden heated it again and
passed it back to the cleaver. She pierced the next mark up on

Flor's back. They did this over and over, with each successive piercing being more painful than the last. Flor held in her vomit. The voice tried a few encouraging words, but all Flor had for it was hatred.

When each mark had been done, the hearth maiden took a hooked knife and placed it in the fire. It glowed bright red when handed to the cleaver. She inserted the tip of it at Flor's belly button and pressing the molten tip to it worked backward, sliced the skin, down to between the labia and up through the buttocks. Flor screamed. The pointers had waited for this and tightened the rope. They were trained to see this pain and to pursue their duty. Flor's agony rippled through the shack. She held nothing but pain and anger.

The final knife was a small, angled thing. Again, the cleaver initiated the cuts at the base of her back and moved on from there up the spine. By this point, Flor could say nothing, she only cried to herself as tears disappeared in the flames below. Working from her stomach, the cleaver took the knife and slowly brought it upward, splitting the skin between her breasts and neck. She ended at her chin.

They paused to let Flor cry and say her final curses. The nearly unventilated shack was filled with smoke. It smelled of herbs and burning flowers that the hearth maiden kept feeding to the fire. She had to make the flames build larger, higher. The highest flame danced just a little below where Flor's naval had been. The heat rose up, cauterizing the open edges of skin.

The cleaver took a breath through her cloth and bent her head to Flor, meeting their foreheads together for a few seconds. It was a sympathetic gesture, a plea for forgiveness. Finally, in a moment that seemed to drag from Flor's infancy to this agonizingly real present, the cleaver ran her knife up the height of her face, over the top of her head, and thus brought the body-encircling wound fully around at last to meet its far terminus at the base of her neck.

A flash occurred and the pointers let go. What was once the body of Flor fell into the fire. In the heat of it, the last of her human vestige, her body, was burned away. The five priestesses dropped to their knees. Rising from the flames was a goddess that looked like Flor, but her hair had grown to wrap itself around her body. She glowed like a lighted lantern.

When everything had gone white, Flor came to know everything. She knew the past that was. She was there the day the deal had been made with her mother. She was there the day the Hickt had conquered the Jel. She was there when a bright little star lit up a lonely planet.

Flor knew the present that was. At the edges of her fingertips she could feel the pulses of every living creature. She could see a child losing her toy in the street across the city. She could feel the last breath of a dying man fields away as if he were breathing on her skin.

She knew the future that would be. Every crumbling building, every shattered bone turning to dust. Every sunrise to come.

For the first time, Flor was whole. Made complete by unspeakable pain and by a bargain made in the name of a dead child. The flames rose around her, her, but she spurned their cocooning grasp, stepped out of them and left the shack. The priestesses went after her.

Ilda had prayed outside the shack, already mourning the loss of her daughter. When the goddess stepped outside, she wanted to run to her and hold her. The face was almost the same. Flor offered her mother a brief glance and a little nod and moved on quickly to a trail that led off toward a nearby hill. The priestesses followed close in her steps behind and Ilda trailed on after them.

The waiting crowd kept their distance. Goddesses were temperamental— without knowledge as to what kind of goddess she was, approaching could be a fatal mistake. At a sufficient distance to view it in its entirety, the goddess that had been Flor turned around and looked out onto the city. She saw it as it had been. She saw what the city was at that moment. She saw the city for what it would be. She pointed a solitary finger at the shack. From her fingertip came a bolt of flame finer than thread, which hit the shack with such power that it lit up the entire building in a moment.

The priestesses looked on in terror, was proof that, alas, she was in fact a destructive goddess. They prayed.

Ilda approached the goddess that had once been held in her daughter. She felt this was her sacrifice to make, having brought this creature into the world. This creature that she could not stop loving no matter how terrible it turned out to be. She looked her in the eyes and asked, "Who are you?"

A smile scrawled itself across the face that looked like Flor's. The goddess went back to gazing at the burning shack and only said, "I am Change, Mother. I am here. I am the Last."

A PROMISE

THE TRACKER DISPLAY READ THAT IT WOULD ONLY BE A matter of hours. Three hours and four seconds, to be exact. Now three. Ilacti found herself tensing up at the prospect. She had started taking the pills days ago in sequence, as instructed, to begin the process. It was easy— each pill and syringe had been laid out and perfectly marked in color-coded packets. The changes had started first in her feet, the edges growing taut and enlarging. She could no longer wear foot coverings. That was fine; she moved very little in the pod.

Then it hit her stomach. She found herself with no appetite and unable to digest anything. She could swallow nothing except liquids and supplements, to further prepare her body for what it would have to do. Then her back became rigid, and she could not lie down. For the last two days she had been unable to sleep anyway, for she would never sleep again. Or she would always be sleeping. She was not clear on which it was.

Ilacti looked at her little pod, littered with photos of her loved ones. In a slab there were the images of her parents, bodies long turned to dust in the great disaster some decades

past. Next to them were the images of her partners, Calagti and
Hull. If she closed her eyes, she could still hear Calagti's golden
laugh, freely given at any moment. If she kept her hand
perfectly still, she could imagine Hull's tender fingers encir-
cling hers. They had all been a good, loving partnership for
each other, each balancing the temperaments of the other. She
missed them, their touch, the sounds of their voices. Even the
way they fought, as would happen on occasion with any relationship. If Ilacti thought too much about it all, she would begin
to cry.

Adjacent to the aforementioned images and covering most
of the walls of her little pod were pictures of her children,
Qwueliu and Monixt, named after their people's names for the
stars. They were why Ilacti was making her way to this distant
place: For them, for their future. Her favorite picture of them
was of the whole family outside on one of the few clear days
left. They had gone to a park, played games and eaten beneath
the trees, struggling to survive. There was a photo of their little
family, dressed for their first day out in ages. The image
captured Monixt's quiet stoicism, even though ze was still a
toddler. There was Qwueliu, eyes upturned and radiating their
perpetual hope. They were her joy, and this, she reassured
herself, was a demonstration of that love.

If Ilacti looked too long at that picture her heart would
ache. She would remember Qwueliu's tears when she informed
them all that she was one of those chosen to leave—that she *had*
to leave. Monixt, still such a small child, had cried silently.
They did not fully understand what was happening, that their
planet was dying. That she was taking on a necessary purpose
which their people had done before when they set sail on their
little world to sparse, once-foreign lands. That dying; that she
was taking on a vital mission; that this would ensure their
survival as a species. She would do anything as a parent to

ensure their survival. The two children only knew they were losing a mother.

On the side of a small table there was a little glass container with a collection of stones her children had given to her. These were the stones had been dug out of the dirt walls of their home. Ilacti was of an age to remember when they first had to go underground. When the gasses had become harsh and the heat from it could fry the skin off a person on especially hot days. It was decided that their people would all move underground. That was cruel fate, for they thrived on sunshine and could only enjoy it when the smog cleared for a few hours in the cold months. She remembered herself as a child, diligently packing away her belongings, leaving her surface home behind for their designated one below the surface.

She could picture her children now, some months after her departure, packing their things. Monixt, especially, would diligently organize zir small toys until each fit in a specialized place in zir suitcase. Qwueliu would have difficulty parting with anything, as ze was a sentimental child. Her children. Children she would not hold again, arranging the small items that had surrounded their lives up to that point.

Ilacti could not form tears anymore, that was part of the changes happening to her body, but she became bleary-eyed looking at the little jar of stones given to her by her children. The stones were from their joint collection. Every time one found an interesting shape or a new color or a particularly shiny stone in the dirt walls of their home, they would pick it out and place it in this special jar. This jar, her photos, and memories were all Ilacti had taken with her.

In just a little under two hours, Ilacti would reach her destination. She closed her eyes and tried to remember her purpose. She remembered the stories of her people, as told to her by her parents: How they had been a nation of travelers, and how their ancient techniques allowed them to settle in any environment. Such was what set them apart from the other beasts, that their physiology could change and adapt the world around them.

The Exodus Incentive was born from this tradition. It was a solution started when she was a child and was only now coming to fruition. They tested the entire adult population for genetic compatibility and then from that pool asked for volunteers. Her notice, that she was one of fourteen possible candidates, had come by courier. Calagti had almost murdered the messenger, for they had all discussed the possible outcome. Any volunteer's family would be set for life, and they would help ensure the survival of their people. Ilacti's purpose was clear, even as her partners cried and begged. Even as Hull could barely speak from it all. Even as their children sobbed, Ilacti would not wait to see her people demolished on a dying planet.

She and four other final volunteers were given their training and directives months ahead of time. The officials had allowed her to choose from one of the available planets. She had picked one that would be seven month's travel, but had a bright, new sun. They had offered to name the planet for her, but she refused. She could not bear her children having to say her name and feel her loss whenever they spoke of where they were traveling. She had suggested they call it "Jhelmb", which in the language of her ancestors meant "warm place". It was accepted.

She had taken the pills at the prescribed times. She injected herself in the correct spots throughout her journey. The chemicals would speed up her body's acclimation and transformation. As she closed to within an hour of her destination, she took the penultimate pill. The others had been bitter, but this she could not taste. Her sense of taste would be the first to leave her, they had said. Ilacti closed her eyes and tried to remember what it was to taste. What it was to taste the sweet summer nectar her people made into delicacies. What was it to the taste of the lips of her partners? Ilacti swallowed her sorrow.

With fifteen minutes remaining in her long journey, the pod's ambient noise became silent. Her hearing had finally gone. They had assured her that would happen at the later stage. She steadied herself against the knowledge that she would never hear the voices of her children again. Looking out through the small window of the pod at the approaching planet, at the place that would eventually house her family, she remembered her purpose.

It was barren, with little atmosphere, but it was not breaking apart the way her home was. There was no vegetation on this new place, on Jhelmb, then again, not much remained on the one she had left behind. Besides, that is what she was here to provide. Ilacti got up and collected her belongings— the photos, the jar. The pod landed. The doors opened out to reveal the rocky, soulless landscape.

Her body was prepared to take the thin atmosphere. She picked a spot and laid her precious little objects around her in a circle and took the last pill. Then she closed her eyes and waited. She thought of the stories her parents had told her as a child of their people: How in a time of great shifts they had traveled to new, inhospitable lands and made them livable through the blood and sacrifice of the strong. Ilacti knew this to be true, for when some of her people bled upon the soil it would enliven for a moment. Dead flowers and plants would bloom anew in the presence of her people's blood

But there was no amount of blood or carnage that would save her dying planet. Not as it was splitting apart in itself. Now they had to search for a home among the stars. All of what was would be dust before long.

In the cool light of the creeping dawn, as her legs rooted

into the ground and her body stiffened, Ilacti wondered if she would still know touch. When her children arrived in a few months, if they put a hand on her, would she feel them? None of the scientists back on her world had ever managed to answer that question, but it hadn't held her back because this wasn't about her, it was about her kind's survival.. She closed her eyes. The sun lit the bark on her face.

PLUM MOON

THERE'S NO AIR. IT'S WHAT ETTA TUVIANO HAD TO KEEP reminding herself. Otherwise, she'd just as easily shirk off her stuffy and all-too-tight helmet and let her dark, thick hair out in the non-atmosphere. It's part of the dream she's always secretly had - nothing separating her from the darkness of space. The cold weightlessness allowing her to move unencumbered. She knew that it was a stupid fallacy. That she would suffocate and freeze to death before she even had the chance to move a finger. But something always led her to gently lay her hand on her helmet trigger when she was waiting for an instruction. [1]

"OK E.T., take the HL3 pipe and insert the tapered end into the 7LM base," Karen's voice buzzed over the intercom. "Oh, and Pierce wants me to remind you that that is our last 7LM base so if it snaps like the last one, we'll be shit out of luck until next month's transit." Etta gingerly began assembling the post, frustrated at the odd angle and poor cut of the piping. "If Pierce doesn't stop giving me shit over that broken pipe, he can come out here and do this himself. Even if I have to drag him out here." They both knew Etta was joking. She loved these exploratory walks, despite the fact that it was menial work.

Karen also reminded her, over the intercom, that "You know how Pierce is, he'd just cry about how women's bodies are just made for these spacewalks. They take the *pressure* better."

"Pierce's body couldn't do anything better," Etta quipped and swallowed her disgust. She paused, having finished the last sets of pieces, to look at the work. It was an odd thing, a combination of a drill and a well that stood out in strong contrast to the surrounding barren moon. Moon XKT-3049D was colloquially referred to as the "Plum Moon" for the heavy concentration of lepidolite that dusted the surface and because early excavations had located a dense, impenetrable core to the body. The Plum Moon revolved around an uninhabitable gas planet (G-XKT) and was a full six month's journey from the closest colony. The only reason the team was out there was to determine if the moon was a good candidate for mining.

Continuous colonial expansion meant that humans had to cannibalize any material they had. Even now, the billions of them were swarming at different ends of that galaxy, eating through planet, moon and asteroid alike. Etta always felt a slight discomfort at the thought of it, even if she was only a tiny part of that machine. But this job was her chance to leave the over-crowded colony in which she had grown up. She looked out at the vastness of the Plum Moon, the still sand punctuated by impossible crystalline formations glowing purple in the muted light of a red sun, and thought of home. She was the only crew member that slept without her window set to opaque just to doze off staring out at the cold, quiet forever.

"Three minutes, E.T. Turn on the thing and get back in here for lunch," Karen said. Etta reluctantly turned on the machine and took one last look at the mostly untouched moon before heading back to their base. Karen met Etta in the depressurization chamber. "Hold it Sparky," she said, holding up a green-lit metal wand. "Scanners detected a foreign body as you walked in." Karen waved the DECT stick over Etta's limbs, looking for that telltale red blink, but no such luck.

"No hitchhiking aliens or is the DECT stick broken?" Etta said with a raised eyebrow.

"Well it sure ain't the DECT stick. I just reviewed this one. Maybe the scanners are on the fritz or maybe you're hiding something from us, E.T.," Karen replied with a wink that made Etta's heart quicken despite herself. Etta stored her suit and they headed for the kitchens to eat with the other team members.

Karen tilted her head to a tall, muscular blonde woman sitting at the end of the oversized metal table. "Scanner's on the fritz G."

"No, it's not. I just checked the specs this morning," Goldie said, looking up from the odd fish-shaped dish she'd been picking at.

Karen gave her a playful shove as she sat down next to Goldie. "Well it's not my DECT stick. I did diagnostics on it just a couple of hours ago."

"Sure. Maybe you've been sticking your DECT stick where it doesn't belong," Goldie said with a mischievous smile.

Karen raised an eyebrow. "Is that a proposition?" she said, flirtation heavy in her face and tone. Her full lips curled up at one end into a smirk.

Etta took that as her moment to turn away from their heavy banter, trying to hide the discomfort she felt. The pair had been bed-warming with one another the last few months, and while both insisted it was a casual affair, Etta could tell otherwise. She had masked her own attraction to Karen since they had met in transit last year, so well that Karen didn't even register it. It was ultimately fine with Etta: watching her closest friend on this far-off rock happily engage with Goldie warmed her heart, if not her bed. What bothered her was the closeness of it all. The way people crowded each other.

Resident physician and nutritionist Rebecca had been coming their way and overheard their conversation. "What's this about the scanners?" she said as she placed plates in front of Etta and Karen, each made to their specific dietary requirements. Rebecca brushed a stray, smooth black hair back behind her ear and sat next to the trio. Her thin, artificially youthful face radiated a calm and restrained curiosity.

"Oh, either the scanner is broken or the DECT stick is and Etta dragged in aliens," Karen said, stuffing a mouthful of starch mash. "The scanners listed a code red but the DECT stick found nothing," she explained, a bit of mash leaving her mouth in the process.

"Or," interrupted Heath from down the table, "Etta's just an alien, and we have to accept our new overlords."

Etta sighed and looked down at her dish, squash composite. "Probably the scanners caught a mote stuck to the suit."

"Mm, not possible," said Goldie. "Scanners read for four different types of radiation signatures. Anything that is cataloged as having been Earth-based biological radiation signatures is registered as default to the machine. It's anything that has a radiation not within parameters that sets it off. But it's got levels. If it's inorganic and radiation levels aren't toxic it's blue. It'll only go red for organic objects with radiation signatures that are non-Earth based."

"OK, so why didn't the DECT stick pick it up? Or do they pick up different information than the scanners?" Heath asked, a boyish bounce to his eating and talking.

Goldie shook her head. "No, DECT sticks are just smaller, more precise versions of the scanners. And they sync data with the scanners. If the scanners picked up something, the DECT sticks would be looking for those signatures."

"Hmmm. Well then," Rebecca said, eyes narrowing in thought, "what could have set off the scanner but not the DECT stick? It'd have to be organic and non-Earth based. Perhaps organic material reached here from an asteroid from somewhere else? Or maybe some of our organic material got out and was irradiated?"

Goldie bit her cheek. "We measure for live organic material, no matter how small. The scanners were developed to prevent the spread of possible alien bacteria that could make explorers sick, or worse, cause an epidemic. Dead organic material doesn't register a red-light warning. And our own materials are compensated for in first planet scan."

"So... aliens?" Karen said with a dramatic wave of her arms.

"Oh come on, a hundred planets plus and never a sign of life," Pierce said, breaking his silent meal. "Aliens are a myth, even alien bacteria."

"Well, I mean, we're not from this moon, so aren't *we* technically the aliens?" said Etta.

"Maybe just you E.T." said Karen, giving Etta a playful poke. Etta tried not to blush.

"You know what I mean. Probably just a scanner misread. Told you to order a new set last week," said Pierce.

Goldie just rolled her eyes until Rebecca intoned "Wouldn't it be curious though?"

"What would be curious?" said Heath.

"Well, a living thing, maybe small like bacteria, or not existing in our field of vision, so for all intents and purposes – invisible. A living thing that would first register as having a non-earthling radiation signature, but quickly adapting to mimic our own radiation. Wouldn't that be strange?" said Rebecca, her eyes pointed in the distance.

. . .

"But why? Why somehow mimic radiation signatures of another being? How would it be capable of that?" said Goldie, a very real concern growing on her face.

"Survival." said Etta. "Think about it, this rock is barren, imitation is a classic survival mechanism. And if you're something small, like a cluster of bacteria, you could do it fast and adapt to a new environment. An organism like that could probably survive any environment."

The room fell silent at the prospect. The hum of the machines that kept them alive in the middle of unforgiving space grew louder with each second.

"That's actually rather frightening," Rebecca said, needing to keep the silence at bay. "I mean, an organism that could imitate another's so well it's almost invisible. Beautiful, but frightening."

"It's only frightening if it develops a taste for Earthlings," said Pierce. "Besides, for it to be any threat it would naturally have to be toxic or a predator or sentient or viral. And as of yet we haven't found sentience on any of these planets. No intelligent life outside what we bring. Leave the creepy impossible aliens to the vid makers. It's more likely that the scanners are on the fritz."

"I'll contact base and get them to send a program patch," said Goldie, aimlessly moving her food on her plate. Karen scooted close to her, perhaps seeking Goldie's warmth or just the comfort of a known body, Karen's dark skin nicely contrasting against Goldie's pale complexion. They resembled a living Yin and Yang.

"Rebecca, why am I eating greenies again? You know I hate this! It tastes like toe fungus!" said Heath. It was clear that Heath was trying to lighten the mood and change the conversation. His effort to alleviate their worries was met with a few chuckles. His tantrum diverted the conversation to a light-hearted one over whether the benefits of greenies was worth the taste. But the discomfort sat in the back of their minds.

* * *

Etta was the only crew member that liked to spend her rec hours on the observation deck. She would have rather spent it in a suit on an outside walk, but when she floated the idea past Karen after they first arrived, she let her know in no uncertain terms she was being an inconsiderate ass.

"Walks need to be monitored by another crew member and they need to check the specs. You're gonna make me or some other sucker spend their rec hours doing that?" Then she bopped Etta's nose with a finger and walked off.

Instead, Etta would bring a workout mat to the Observation Deck to take in the views from the safety of the compound. It was a small, domed structure, where the walls were made from a high-density clear plastic resin, partitioned by steel. It was the space version of a glass house. The exposure of the setup made more than one crew-member uncomfortable to be in there for too long. Heath had mentioned once that if he stayed on the observation deck for more than twenty minutes, he felt like he couldn't breathe. He kept imagining that the walls would break and he would die in space, his breath sucked straight out of his body.

For Etta it was an opposite feeling. Etta relished the openness of it. She could almost see herself walking through the walls and out into the landscape. Between the interior walls and wearing her helmet outside of them, she was suffocating. This was her only release.

Etta tried to normalize her being there by bringing the mat.

Rebecca liked to come in her morning hours and meditate. But Etta's focus was not on centering her body or perfecting her form. She used this as a vehicle to stare out into the great, purple-tinted desert. She could see the last vestiges of the system's red sun's rays as it set off the moon's horizon. The red light made for a magenta glow coming off the still dust of the moon. It caused the large stone formations to trail long shadows. Black figures that lay on the ground.

This was Etta's second assignment. Her first had been three years ago on the water planet H749. It was a planet much like Earth 1 in temperament and size. It already had an atmosphere and needed minimal terraforming. After their surveying, the company decided it would be billed as a Pleasure Planet. By now the "life" would have been introduced and hotel after hotel would have been built making H749, now "IndiSea", the ultimate tourist attraction.

That had been where she'd first met Karen. Karen still referred back to that planted paradise. She would regularly reply that instead of being stuck on this rock she could be sunbathing or surfing at IndiSea.

Etta had enjoyed H749 when she had first arrived, but could not see herself there now. She loved the Plum Moon more. It was just everything she had dreamed of as a child. The foreignness of it. The danger. It was much more *alien*. It was that much more *beautiful*.

She reflected on this as she sat still watching the shadows grow longer. She was almost sure that it was the light when she thought she saw something *move*.

* * *

Look at you Etta, still getting spooked by shadows, she said to herself, as she laid down in her bed to sleep that night. She turned the dials at the wall of her bed cupboard to set her preferred mattress temperature. This was the worst part of the day for Etta; trying to get to sleep in the coffin-like bed was an anxiety-ridden battle each evening. She never understood why the engineers and designers had made their sleeping pods incredibly small. According to Goldie, it was because crew rooms were supposed to double as escape pods in original designs, and that they had hoped the sleeping pods could eventually be swapped out for stasis chambers. That is if the costs for stasis chambers ever came down.

Etta was very sure she would rather die in an explosion, like the one that killed the colonists of Helofax29, than spend an indeterminate amount of time in a stasis chamber. Cramped in the six and a half foot, by three and a half foot, by two-foot chamber was the stuff of her continued nightmares. The only comfort was her small port window looking out into the vastness of purple plains. She angled herself so that her face was close to the high-density plastic. She imagined she was out there, in the incredible lightness of it. Her bare feet planted in the violet soil. Freedom surrounding her body. Those fantasies nursed her to sleep.

That night, the crew remained restless, as if something was perpetually disruptive. There was the soft, almost noiseless ting-ting-ting outside Rebecca's room, like pebbles falling on metal. The *ping, ping, ping* pried her from out of her slumber the entire night. She would begin to slide into sleep when a ping would jolt her awake. Or, she'd be in the middle of a repetitive dream when a ping would insert itself there and jolt her upright, whereupon she'd once again hit her head on the top of the chamber.

There was the sudden change in air pressure in Goldie's quarters that woke up Karen, gasping and choking. When Goldie checked the stats, everything read in normal parameters. Neither Heath nor Pierce would admit to their nightmares. Both had dreams that they were paralyzed and suffocating.

Etta also felt something, an imperceptible hum that none of the instruments picked up on. It threw the universe just off rhythm. A steady buzzing, like cicadas in summer. Except this buzzing missed a beat every few hundred beats. It was almost like something was sending a signal.

What most don't know about deep space travel is that people depend on consistency. They depend on routine to give the illusion of safety. In the broadest terms, deep space travel carries dangers that could give even the bravest a sudden panic attack when they consider that they're sending out a group of people into the near unknown with just a tin can around them to prevent them from the endless expanse of the universe. Unless a planet has been terraformed or altered for human habitation, it's just a few centimeters of plastic and metal between a crew and oblivion. Quiet is good. Consistency is good. Any deviation from those things brings the reminder that they are alone. With every clip of a stray rock flying in space, every wrong instrument reading brings back the fear.

For all that, breakfast was uncharacteristically quiet. Heath attempted a few halfhearted jokes to lighten the mood but it did little to alleviate the pensive stillness in the station. The crew mostly pushed around their food around on their plates. Even Rebecca, who tended to be dogmatic about proper nutrition, only picked at her carbohydrate combination. The sole exception was Etta, who was ravenous to the point where the rest of the crew gave her their leftovers. She gulped them down with fury. Rebecca was too focused on her lack of sleep to take note of Etta's appetite even though she had also given the woman her leftovers. Etta swallowed each morsel but was left hungry and unsatisfied. She quelled her complaints for their morning meeting.

"I got the service specs on the scanners and DECT sticks. Everything checks out," Goldie started. "The only stuff that got through was the typical matter."

"Then what was the missed alarm?" said Karen, rubbing her eyes. She hadn't been able to fully sleep after that choking incident, even after she'd left Goldie's quarters in a huff.

"Just a blip. No machine is perfect. Could have also misread Etta for a second before it re-registered," said Goldie, with a calm that seemed forced. She and Karen's late-night fight had left a sour taste in both their mouths.

"Speaking of blips, we may want to check if there are any asteroid showers coming soon. That could explain the pebbles hitting near my room last night," said Karen.

"I can get to that after lunch. In the meantime, we've gotten odd readings on the drill. Etta, are you up for a walk?" Pierce waited until Etta nodded enthusiastically before continuing. "And Goldie you're gonna need to see if the readings are another mechanical issue." Goldie nodded and picked her teeth with a ring finger. "And Karen, I'm going to need you to double check all the math by hand."

Karen answered with a sarcastic salute and an "Aye Aye Captain."

"Heath, can you begin assembling the aperture for the digger and pump?" Pierce continued.

"Sure, but I'm still waiting for the second half of parts from TaramX5. They won't be here for another four days," said Heath.

"Just do what you can until then. Everyone have their assignments?" Pierce didn't even look up from his tablet to check if people were still paying attention. "Meeting adjourned. Dismissed."

Etta had to deliberately slow her walk as she rushed to the suit chamber. Despite her head getting to her after that shadow she saw, she felt an urgent need to leave the domed enclosure and feel the sand beneath and between her toes. She would have to settle for the sand beneath a boot instead. Etta emerged with the suit uncomfortably tight and loose at the same time. Her breath felt caught and labored beneath all the layers, the thick fabric further inhibiting her movement. The stuffiness reminded her of how her mother would tightly tuck her inside her sheet and cotton comforter. After her mother left, she would throw them off and sleep naked in the summer or the winter. In this suit she was bundled in those covers again, but now she had to maneuver.

While Etta was fidgeting with her arm straps a voice came over the intercom. "Etta, read one?" It was Pierce, testing the coms. "Yeah. I read. Isn't Karen going to be my second?" She went right back to fixing her straps when Pierce reminded her that Karen would be doing math for most of the day. "Everyone else is busy," said Pierce, preempting her next question.

The half-light came on and Etta became even more interested in finishing getting ready and getting out there. Pierce walked into the transfer chamber to check her straps and fittings. There was always something about the way he ran his hands over the straps, the way his eyes looked at her in these close quarters, that bothered her. He was following the rules to a "T" but that didn't mean that while he was fitting her, his finger didn't "accidentally" caress a nipple, the side of a breast, the arch of a buttock or the space between her thighs.

This had started three months ago, and the first time he did it, Etta had earnestly thought it was an accident. While clicking a side suit link, his hand went and cupped her beneath her breast. He made it seem like a slip while he made sure the fasteners were tight enough. But then it kept happening, and each time he was bolder about it than the last. Etta looked at the camera footage later and noted with dismay that he had angled himself in such a way that nothing was discernible. She also remembered that as the lead on these projects, he had the camera access code and could probably delete anything if necessary.

There were several occasions where she had tried to broach the subject with the other crewmembers, but she had to be extremely careful. Any accusation could get her fired in one way or another. Above that, no one else seemed to have this issue with him. Then again, she was the one who did the majority of the walks. The rest of the crew already found her "odd," who would believe her anyway? Even Karen, for all her wry humor about Pierce, hadn't noticed anything.

As soon as her helmet was buckled and she'd mentally zoned out from the unwanted molestation, Etta bolted to the chamber. Her tank and backpack strapped, she grabbed the bag of tools near the exit shelf. "Ready," she said over the intercom, waiting for Pierce to make his way into the control booth to press the open sequence. "Ready," he said after only a minute's time, but it felt like an eternity to her.

She could almost feel his breathing as he kept the com open and it made her want to vomit. "We are live Etta. Depressurizing at 25%. Going 'green' in 3, 2, 1."

The doors opened, and that day seemed even more beautiful than the day before. Another of G-XKT's moons was close by in orbit. If this was the Plum Moon, that was the Silver one. It was next to be drilled and surveyed because the Silver Moon had mercury deposits. But for now, it was peaceful, reflecting a gray light from its surface to the plum moon. It drowned the landscape in lilac.

With her first step off the platform, she felt it. That vibration she had felt the entire night before. It was faint, like a tickle traveling from the sole of her boot upwards to her ankles and thighs. Everything seemed to register the tingle. It was arrhythmic, uneven. If Etta hadn't known better, she'd have been tempted to say it was a language. But she did know better and she had done some before-breakfast reading on the subject of vibrations and how bodies in space have sometimes been affected by the gravitational pulls of multiple satellites. At least this was the conclusion in one or two theories.

Anyway, putting such thoughts out of her head, she looked eight meters forward to the drill. A few more steps along and she was striding in time with the mysterious sounds. *A song,* Etta thought. *It reminds me of a song but I don't know what song or where I have heard it.* She muted her com to hum along. With every step she took she began to dance along to it, hopping and tapping, letting the distorted rhythm move her. She was happy there were no station cameras at this distance.

On the surface, the drill looked exactly as she had left it. She turned on her helmet camera and checked the monitoring systems first. She heard Pierce come through and turned on both her com and the unit.

"OK, I'm reading interference about one hundred and forty-five meters down. What does it look like to you?" Pierce's voice came over like a static mess. The sound of it, close and in her ear, made her sweat.

"Checking now," she said, as she peered at the scope. It wasn't stuck at the one-forty-five mark, it had made it eighteen more meters before the safety shutdown had kicked in. The drill was really just to do more in-depth surveying and sample collecting, and machines like that tended to be "wheat stalks" as Heath called them. They were compact and light for space travel, and had some flexibility, but too much pressure and they snapped. She noted at the one-hundred forty-five it hit a thicker patch of material and programed the side arm to take a sample. There was another patch farther down where it had finally stopped.

"I'm seeing a thicker deposit, looks like harder rock vein at those levels," Etta said over the com.

"That's impossible," Pierce replied.

Etta rolled her eyes, "I'm just telling you what I see. There's thicker material down here. Looks like strands of compact sheeting."

"And I'm telling you that the bot that surveyed this moon found no hard veining, it's the reason it was pushed up on the mining catalog. Easy access to materials and all that."

"I'm just telling you what I see."

"OK. Just program it to bring up samples," Pierce said.

"Already on it," Etta had to work to keep the annoyance out of her voice. "Listen, it's going to take like an hour at least for these samples to come up -"

"Do you want to come back?" Pierce interrupted.

"No." Etta shuddered at the thought of having him unwrap her only to have him wrap her back up an hour later. "I'm going to do some surveying, see if I find anything interesting."

"The previous team already did layouts of everything."

"Might not be a waste. I've got two hours, forty-three minutes in the air pack. I'm muting to concentrate and not break the suit," she said and did just that before Pierce could respond. Etta looked at the counter and saw that it would be approximately an hour and a quarter before it had to be checked. Standing up, she looked at the landscape, drenched in the eerie, reflected light. Lost in that landscape, wanting more senses in on the moment, she drew in a deep breath...only to realize halfway through that it was just recycled oxygen from her suit. It was instinctual, the type of breath someone might make when they first got on holiday at the seaside. But there were no breaths to be had without the helmet. There was no air to smell.

She pondered what the air might have smelt like, had the moon any sort of atmosphere. The color obviously begged for a hint of lavender. If the company had selected this moon for a tourist destination, she imagined that the tele-ads would reference the "Lavender Sky and Amethyst Sands." But then, something reminded her of the plumeria plant her mother kept alive back home. The delicate smell of it, the very "purpleness" of it spoke to her. Like when she had been just a child screaming and running in the garden, looking at the flowers; pointing to the sky.

Etta picked a direction to explore. The rock formations just to her left and about sixty meters off seemed interesting. Feeling the rhythm that pulsed beneath her, she danced her way to them. She hummed in along with the tune, her high voice matching the melody of the moon's low, quiet octave. Approaching a large mass, she tilted her head back. It reminded her of dried, dark calcified coral left on the beach, portions sculpted smooth by the endless movement of the tide, while other regions retained their pitted features.

These were not like the formations of her home planet, which had been birthed by volcanic activity and eroded into existence. These were the remains of an asteroid shower that had bombarded the moons and the planets here a millennium ago. Once upon a time, they used to call objects like that shooting stars, but these were like bullets or arrows, embedding themselves into the flesh of this moon, projectiles that had flown through space only to explosively become lodged on a little forgotten rock.

When Etta stepped away from the cluster of meteors, she noted that it resembled a hand. At very least, the five "rocks" looked like five fingers stretching, reaching out from beneath the ground. She took a photo with the lab-cam. She may as well have some memento from this assignment. At the click of the image she felt a quake. Nothing dangerous, just a quiver from beneath, as if the moon was settling itself.

Etta got her bearings and moved slightly to her left. At this angle it looked as if the hand formation was reaching for the silvered sister moon. She took another photo and the moon quivered with more intensity. She fell and felt the deep rumbling. It was foreboding, but also seductive. She remained prone there until it finally stopped a moment later.

She checked her suit and its stats: The urgency red light on the com was blinking and she turned it on.

"Etta! Etta! Do you read? Are you there?" Pierce was panicked. A dead crewman could be a career end.

"Yes, I'm fine. Suit is fine, pack is fine. I'm heading to check on the drill and the samples."

"Forget it. Come back to base. I'll send Heath out later to collect the samples." Pierce's voice was more urgent than she'd ever heard. "You have to get Rebecca to look you over, it's text-book regulation. Suit censor registered an impact."

From when I fell, but she omitted that tidbit. The last thing she wanted was to be docked from walks until an injury profile was done. She only glanced at the drill on her way back, it seemed fine. When she turned around for one last look at the formation, she could have sworn that the five clustered "fingers" seemed to have somehow bent at their "joints" to resemble a hand even more.

* * *

"Look at the light." Rebecca had already measured anything there was to measure, and was still doing tests. Blood profiles, temperature, heart rate, bladder and stool samples. Etta was growing impatient with it, but she could also tell that Rebecca was being thorough as a distraction. The entire crew was quite literally trembling from the quake when she came back.

"Stick out your tongue again." Rebecca put the tongue depressor on Etta's tongue and looked back at her notes. She'd done everything twice at this point and Etta was tired of being poked and prodded. "What's the prognosis Doc?" Etta said in a forced jovial voice.

"Oh," Rebecca said, seeming to snap out of her stupor. "You're fine but I want you on rest for one cycle just to be safe. And your temperature is a little low. Not enough to merit any meds, but I want you to wear this ring thermometer for the day. It'll send me your updated temps wirelessly to keep track. Don't take it off, not even when you shower."

Etta fingered the plain silver band that encircled her middle finger. For what looked like plain metal it felt oddly warm. She left the exam room and headed toward the kitchens and dining area. Taking a sweetened fruit drink cocktail from the snack stores, she spotted Karen bent over some tablets at the open kitchen table. Etta peered over her shoulder at the various equations and formulas, then sat down next to her.

Karen just nodded in acknowledgment of her new company. After a few moments and calculations, she finally addressed Etta. "*You're* awfully calm there E.T., even though you were out there."

"I guess I wasn't near anything that was shaking or falling off walls to get scared by."

"Or maybe that isn't the only thing to be afraid of," Karen said under her breath. Realizing Etta had probably heard it, she turned to her with wide eyes.

Etta answered her with a quizzical look. Karen shook her head at the tablets in front of her. "It's just... it doesn't make sense. None of these stats match to the projections and calculations the first team did. I haven't seen unpredictability like this since I did predator migrations in my internship, and those things were alive! I just..."

Etta put a hand on Karen's shoulder. It was a tentative gesture, and for all their familiarity, one that felt forced. The buzzing of the station seemed too still while Etta pondered what had changed, how this woman whom she had been attracted to seemed like a stranger to her suddenly. "I'm sorry it's frustrating. What do you think it could be?"

"I... I don't know. I mean, this isn't normal. These tremors aren't normal for a moon like this. These readings make no sense and it's the one thing that should make sense out of any of it. I keep running through them and all I hear is my mom's old ghost stories in my head!" Karen slammed one hand on the table and ran the other across her shorn hair.

"Ghost stories?"

"Yeah, I... my mother believed in ghosts and hauntings and I... I've never grown out of it."

Etta forced a chuckle, but it was hollow. That feeling of a presence had also been in the back of her mind. She didn't feel haunted, just not alone. Etta looked away, but saw nothing there.

"I know! I know! It's just," Karen's breath was quickening

"No one has been able to prove whether ghosts are real or not and I just-I don't know what to make of this. I don't know what to make of the change in the air and the weird stuff."

"I know it's scary, but it's probably just old equipment," Etta said, trying to sound logical in the face of her own blooming unease.

Karen rubbed her shoulder, "Remember what happened on Helofax29? The investigation found that the crew ignored warning signs. Like, strange happenings and all that? What if that's happening here?"

"We aren't ignoring the weird stuff though, I mean you're here checking the math," Etta said.

"It's this feeling I have though. Like something else. It's – well – alien. Ghostly."

"Alien? Do you mean?"

Before Etta could finish, they were interrupted by the emergency alarm. The siren's screeching reflected in Karen's eyes, wide with fear. She looked at Etta as if to say "told you so". Instead they heard Pierce's voice over the intercom, telling the entire crew to head to the Exit Chamber, and they both rushed out of their seats.

The scene was chaos. Heath was in a walking suit screaming and kicking on the floor. Goldie had gotten to the area before them, and she was holding him down on the ground by his shoulders. Rebecca had the med kit open on the floor, searching for something inside. Pierce was at Heath's side, undoing the straps to loosen the suit. Rebecca looked up to see Karen and Etta and screamed at them to help hold him down. Karen launched herself to Heath's left arm and sat on it. Etta headed towards his kicking legs and held them down. Then she saw it, on his right calf: Something had pierced the suit. Karen located the needle she had been looking for and Pierce had unlatched a portion of the breast of the suit. Karen stuck the needle in and Heath stopped fidgeting, put to sleep by the sedative.

"What in the hell happened?" Karen screeched.

Rebecca licked her lips and took a breath. She was taking another look through the med case. "Heath was out there retrieving the samples: On his way back a foreign object, debris probably, went through the suit. Didn't get to his skin, but through about most of the layers by the look. He was still able to get back in but he started going into shock the minute we closed the doors."

She took a small pair of scissors and cut away at the layers of fabric, but before she had finished Etta could see that there was a small cut, barely the size of a fingernail, deep in the skin. It had impacted him, and now there was risk of exposure. The area around the cut was bluish-black. Rebecca injected the site with her other needle and brushed herself off. "We need to get him to the med sector."

Goldie, Pierce and Karen lifted Heath and hauled his limp form out. Rebecca grabbed the case and followed. Etta looked after them, rooted in place by the strange feeling that had come over her: She felt as though she was watching the scene with two sets of eyes. One set was wholly hers, horrified at the possibility of Heath losing a limb. The other set watched the scene with detachment of watching an experiment play out. It was a set of eyes that felt *alien*.

Etta couldn't remember how she had gotten to Heath's room or why she was there. She looked around, noting the pictures he had taped to the walls of his small enclosure. The collected set of creature cards and decks that he kept on a small shelf. He was always trying to get someone to play, but so far hadn't fully convinced any of the crew members to play. She zeroed in on the picture of Heath as a child above the entrance to his bunk. In the photo, his eyes were still alight with innocent glee. His mother's out-of-fashion haircut framed a warm and welcoming face. His sister, the spitting image of him, had the same sweet smile. He must have been around seven in the picture. How old was he now? She had never had the occasion to ask.

That's about when she remembered that she was there to check his preferred bed settings. According to Rebecca, they were to make Heath as comfortable as possible while he recovered. And he would recover, she assured everyone, despite the graze and the exposure. But for all that, Etta had a strange feeling of foreboding.

After taking the preference readings, Etta headed back to the med center. The space was little more than a slightly larger crew quarter, with every single inch devoted to medical equipment. The quarter had been reconfigured to have the bed in the center, and fully stripped of everything, Heath lay asleep and sedated there. Rebecca was typing notes on a pad to the right when Etta entered. Etta typed in and re-set the bed settings, but when she turned to go Rebecca stopped her.

"I want to thank you, Etta." Rebecca's face was drained and pallid. Her voice came out pained, as if it were sliding over shards of glass.

"For what?" Etta replied.

"For not, well, not calling me out on my little white lie. I know you could see the injury, but I really didn't want anyone else to panic. We already had Heath in shock, I was trying to keep everyone calm." She could not look directly at Etta.

She took her index and middle fingers and rubbed her right eye. The slowness of movement spoke for itself: Rebecca was breaking.

Etta nodded while those alien eyes she now felt she had overlooked Heath. A voice that was hers made its way out. "Do you think he is going to be okay? Really?"

"I don't know. I think so. I hope so. But he was three meters away from the entrance when he was struck. I honestly don't know how he made it back before he froze or suffocated or both. Whatever hit him was small, thankfully." She leaned back and rubbed her neck. Her eyes slid to Heath, and Etta could sense it, the burden that Rebecca took on being their doctor on these trips. The terrible thought that no matter the cause, no matter the issue, you could never remain blameless.

"We're pulling shifts to monitor Heath. Yours will start in two hours, please be back here," Rebecca said with finality. Etta replied with a nod.

* * *

Goldie had brought in the samples Heath had dropped near the entrance, and Pierce had locked himself away to analyze them. Karen worked in her quarters, poring over the figures with more maddening precision. A perpetual anxiety had draped over the base, such that it was filled with an unusual and eerie silence. Etta tuned the silence out, and concentrated on the low hum she still seemed to hear as she walked back into the med center in time for her watch.

Rebecca looked up from her screen at hearing Etta's footsteps and showed her a wounded expression and she heavily lifted herself from her seat.

Etta broke the silence that ensued. "How's he doing?"

"No change, except he seems to have an... I'll call it an infection. It's best to keep him sedated. I've sent the results to our nearest med team at Oraxis satellite and they are going over what I've found."

"Infection?"

Rebecca pursed her lips and looked at Heath's body, a slow breathing corpselike thing. "Yes. But it's best not to make much of this. I think he'll keep his leg but his body needs rest. Alert me of any changes. I'm gonna get something to eat. Need anything before I go?" The offer's sincerity didn't reach her face.

Etta shook her head, and with that Rebecca dragged herself out of the room.

They were alone. Or more properly, with Heath sedated in the bed, his leg restrained by an old frayed seat belt that had been re-purposed into a tourniquet, Etta was alone. The monitors and machines Heath was hooked up to punctuated the silence with the steady beats of his stats. Unable to resist her curiosity, she went over hoping to get a look at his wounded leg, but it was tightly bound and bandaged.

Etta noted that Rebecca had lowered the light settings, probably to create a more soothing mood, but all it did was begin to lull her to sleep. She suspected that may have been why Heath's fair complexion was taking on a bluish-purple tone.

Sitting down, Etta tried to kill time by reading an old book on her tablet, but found her mind too eager to concentrate. She settled on her old hobby, and clarified the window settings to look out at the landscape. The Plum Moon currently happened to be at just the right angle with respect to the system's star such that the view she was seeing mimicked a sunset. The light was crawling down the horizon. Etta daydreamed about walking out in that sand, free of everything that held her. Soon her eyes had closed and the machines hummed to Heath's heartbeat.

· · ·

It wants you.

Etta woke, but was paralyzed. She hadn't even realized that she had fallen asleep at the small desk.

It wants you.

Her mind was awake, but her body was plastered to itself. That voice came from her side, from Heath's body. But it was not him.

It wants you.

She finally moved, each limb as heavy as stone, and stood straight up. Heath's body was the same, plastered, unmoving. But his eyes and mouth were open. Etta approached him, and saw that his machines were the same as they had been, his stats normal for sedated patient.

It wants you.

The voice croaked. It was Heath, his lips moving in a slow, disjointed spasms. As she came closer, she could see his eyes. But they were not his eyes. Those eyes had lost all their luster and gone milky. She had only seen eyes like that a handful of times before. They were the eyes of a corpse.

It wants you.

Drool escaped his mouth.

"Heath?" Etta put a hand gingerly on his. She wanted to calm him in case this was a symptom of shock. Or if the infection had blinded him.

His head turned, slowly. Etta swore she heard a creak at the movement. *Etta... it wants you.* Gone was that voice with the boyish lift. What came out was rocky, gravel on steel.

"Heath? Heath, can you hear me?" The white-eyed thing looked at her. "Who? Who wants me?" Her lips became a thin line.

It does. It ... knows you. You know it.

Etta slowly lifted her hand, ready to hit the alarm. This was clearly something Rebecca needed to see. Before she reached the alarm button, however, Heath sat straight up, tearing the restraints. He grabbed her upper arms in his surprisingly strong hands. He squeezed her until it hurt.

She tried to shake out of his grip, but he looked her in the eye. There was something dark oozing from the corners of his eyes, mouth and from his nose. His gaze petrified her and he brought her face close in to his own.

"Let me go! Heath! Stop!" She didn't want to drop an injured man on the floor by pulling him off the table, but she was frightened. This was not some "infection". It was more. He looked possessed.

He opened his mouth, more viscous ooze coming forth and screamed, "TAKE ME OUTSIDE! NOW!"

Etta screamed at the sight. He threw her with a strength that Heath had never exhibited before. Her body crashed and crumpled against a wall. Aching, she managed to get up off the floor and hit the wall alarm as he bolted from the room, blackish-purple liquid seeping from his wound. Etta crawled to the doorway to see Heath running down the hall towards the exit doors. "Stop him!" she screamed, ribs aching with the movement.

Pierce came out of nowhere and tackled Heath to the ground.

They watched in horror as Heath's legs dissolved into a puddle beneath him, followed by his torso and arms, melting into that goo. Pierce rolled over Heath's melting body. He grabbed at Heath, his hands grasping at the dissolving flesh and only coming up with the thick, violet ooze. Heath's head looked up at Pierce, his earlobes dripping like melted wax. With his jaw deteriorating, Heath coughed his last words: "It'll take you all..." What was once Heath's head had become a purple gelatinous mass. His last few syllables came out as popped bubbles from the liquid.

There would not be enough of his body left to pack and mail to his parents.

Rebecca's eyes were bloodshot. She had never lost a crewman before. The very sight of him reduced to a puddle of goo, his uniform soaked with liquified entrails, would haunt her forever. It may have been the failure that drew Rebecca down.

She had been the one to locate the infection and assumed it benign. Now she wouldn't make that mistake again: Through Pierce, they now had a quarantine order. They had alerted the closest patrol base and a team was on the way.

It was a standing evacuation order, but it would still take four days for the shuttle to arrive. Until then, everyone had to stay put. Rebecca even went as far as wearing a hazmat suit to treat Etta's fractured rib. Her pale face was tinted green beneath the visor as she worked to set the cast to deal with the fracture.

She didn't ask about Etta's pain or discomfort and Etta didn't offer any such feedback. Rebecca had already taken blood samples from the crew to assess if anyone else had been infected or exposed. But even Rebecca confessed that she couldn't be sure that it had been that particular infection that had caused it.

The name "Heath" had become prohibited in conversation. No one wanted to remember his last moments, his body dissolving into no more than spilled syrup. Goldie, the only one who had the stomach for it, was silently forced to scrape up his remains from the floor.

Etta was unnerved by the whole scene. Pierce watched from a distance while Goldie hunched with a scraper and a bucket. *Pierce should be doing that,* she thought, remembering how he had been the one to fully tackle an injured Heath. The scene kept replaying in her mind. *He should have been the one,* she thought again and again, trying to superimpose Pierce's face over Heath's as he melted.

Rebecca finished setting Etta's bandages. With a full dosage of painkillers, she sent Etta on her way. She was to come back to Rebecca after she woke up. Walking back to her room, Etta was discomforted by the disquieting noise of the base. It was typically quiet, but then, as not a soul was permitted within breathing distance of another, the pumped automated air was more still than usual. The station was a ghost town, with people squatting in its haunts.

There was a peace to the quiet, but it bothered Etta enough that she was glad for the pills that quickly put her to sleep. As her eyelids drifted downward, tugged by the artificial drowsiness, she realized she could feel that offbeat hum that seemed to follow her outside. She hummed along with it, but added something new. She spelled out her name in Morse code to the rhythm.

There was a touch, there in the darkness of a dreamless sleep. It was a phantom breeze that came across her forehead. She instinctively recoiled from it. Etta did not want to be touched by someone else, or something else, when she could not fully move her body. She felt the fear rise subconsciously. Paralyzed in her sleep she could not move from the thing that just grazed her. The breeze pulled back.

Etta could hear something, something in her that went directly into her inner ear. It was a steady, slow beat, and above it, her name in Morse code. It asked her, not with words but with something internal, something unspoken: to see inside. It asked to know her, to sense her. It was a tendril, tentatively asking for permission.

Etta, hearing that rhythm, knew the sound of it slowly uncoiling. It did not ask, but it tiptoed its questions. Etta showed herself to it, she showed her life with her mother. She showed it her exploits as a child, running amok in her backyard yearning for freedom that those bound by their world could not feel. She showed it her school and the people she fell in and out of love with.

The thing slowly dug deeper, easing into her thoughts and her memories. It unwillingly saw the times when Pierce's hands roamed about her body. It recoiled at the feeling of violation. Then after a few other pleasant memories, of being outside, it was the memory of Etta's rib crushed by the impact of Heath's push. Something wiggled above her skin, down her collarbone, between her breasts and to the bandaged rib. It lingered there, a comforting, invisible touch.

Twelve hours later, Etta woke up and stretched. She had not felt that well rested in the months she had been traveling. Then it hit her-she had no pain in her chest. Panicked, with the fear that her convulsive stretch had unset the broken rib, and that she had not felt it from the painkillers, Etta rang Rebecca.

Rebecca made Etta put on her containment suit before seeing her in the small clinic fifteen minutes later. Rebecca chewed on her lips with the results on both sets of scans. "Impossible," she murmured to herself as Etta lay on the table.

"Did I do something?" Etta asked, trying to feel for any lingering pain. There was none. And in fact, she had a pleasant tingle around the wound. Etta had woken up feeling better than she had in the years she had taken this job. She felt more full, stronger than she had felt in a long time.

"Well," Rebecca began, "I- I don't know what's happened, but those fractures are gone."

"What?"

"They must have been shallower than the scans said. But you're completely healed. Here, I need to take a sample." Rebecca took to Etta's side. She put Etta's arm in an isolation chamber along with a filled hypodermic, positioned herself at the chamber's arm controls and prepared to inject the shot. The needle neared her forearm and Etta instinctively clenched, only to see the needle tip to break against her skin. Rebecca didn't try to disguise her annoyance as she reset with a new needle. This second try she had barely broken the skin when the needle shattered. But before she could reset the whole apparatus for a third time, the alarm rang.

The signal was from the com center. The accompanying message featured nothing more than just a heavy, croaked "Help" climbing through static.

As they got up to head to com center, Etta looked at her arm. Rebecca had broken the skin, and a little bead of blood had formed on the surface. It was purple.

A strange calm came over Etta, who didn't rush off toward the command center like Rebecca but instead simply followed at an unhurried pace.

* * *

Etta met up with Goldie and Karen as they headed to the other side of base. Karen's eyes were bloodshot, either from a lack of rest or from crying. Etta couldn't fully distinguish under the hazmat suits. What she could see was the way Goldie reached over and slipped her hand into Karen's. It was a warm and intimate gesture, something done between two people who weren't just bed-warming for one another. Karen's thumb ran over Goldie's. Together.

There was no jealousy for Etta, just the recognition that they were there for one another in this nightmare scenario. Whatever happened to one of them would happen to the other.

Rebecca was banging on the com door and screaming. Panic had set in. Pierce was inside and he was not opening up. The alarm blared on and on, and the red emergency lights had come on in response. Karen screamed his name and turned to the group.

"He may have passed out! We need to get in!" Rebecca could not lose another crewman.

Goldie pushed her way past and located a side door panel. She peeled it open and after fidgeting with a wire and a pad for a second, she rushed to the door. Goldie pressed her weight on it and began to push, and the door slowly slid. Karen went to her side, and together, as metal screeched against metal, they opened the door to the com center.

Rebecca ran inside as soon as the gap was large enough, and screamed. The rest squeezed one at a time through the small opening to see Pierce. He had been sitting in a chair when it happened, a hand up on a control panel, a fingertip hovering atop the panel's alarm button. Somehow, he had been encased in crystal. They could see his body beneath it all, his face frozen in pain, but it was distorted. The jaw was cartoonishly unhinged and to the side. His eyes bulged out of their sockets.

Whatever had been done, it had not been kind. It had been slow enough for him to feel it, to sound the alarm, but not slow enough to have escaped. The pain was etched beneath the purple-tinged crystal in every misshapen joint, every line in his expression.

Rebecca and Karen went into shock at the sight. Goldie held on to Karen, to give her some strength. Etta only felt a lingering pleasure, and the tug of a smile on her lips that she kept subdued.

"How? How... how how how how how?" Rebecca had collapsed on the floor, her voice broken. Two of the crewman dead.

"Could it be the infection?" Goldie's warm, deep voice cut through it all.

"Yes...no. I don't know!" Rebecca's voice was more haunted beneath the hazmat suit. "I've never seen anything like this! It's there and then it isn't. It disappears, it reappears. We all have it! We're all GOING TO DIE!"

Karen's sobbing cut through the silence. Goldie held her tighter and continued, "What if there's a cure? Something to stop the spread? I mean that team is coming, yes?"

Morbid laughter was Rebecca's first response—a deep, gruesome sound. "You think they are going to cure us? No. No no no no. They'll come here and quarantine us and study how we die! It moves too fast to cure!" And she just laughed, and it echoed on the metal walls of the base, reflecting a distorted version.

Karen looked at Etta, and then back at Rebecca. She straightened her chin and back. "We'll find a way, Rebecca. No one else has shown symptoms."

"It's this place! Don't you see? The purple! It's this godforsaken moon! It's doing this! It's killing us! Well fuck it! I'm going to go down swinging!" With a frantic and desperate expression Rebecca pushed her way past them to the hallway and headed to the burner.

Goldie and Karen bolted after her. Etta paused, feeling a tendril of something tickle her ear. It was speaking to her, coaxing her and asking her to follow. Her legs moved on their own, helped by the persuasion of it.

The "Burner" was the central hub of any station. It was built first, taken down last and always done by a specialist team. As space exploration had crossed galaxies, humans had found that the best source of energy, autonomous and long-lasting was nuclear. The "Burner" was a centrifuge hooked to a nuclear reactor, and once you set it, you were supposed to forget it. Rebecca had remembered it. They found her playing with the maintenance controls, mumbling to herself.

Karen's voice was soft as she approached her. "Rebecca, what are you doing?"

"We're all gonna die anyway," Rebecca said between sobs, hands pushing any button with haphazard abandon. "I'm going to take this place with me."

A nerve struck Etta. She was planning on blowing up the moon, her moon. *Her Life.* She tackled Rebecca to the ground with a strength that was unfamiliar. Goldie tried to pull her off, but it took both her and Karen manage the feat, and even then, they had to work at it for more than a few seconds. Goldie had scratched Etta in the process, but in all the commotion nobody noticed the strange purple hue of her blood right away.

Rebecca wept on the floor. "Don't you see? We have it. The team isn't coming to rescue us, they are coming to contain us. They'll kill us here if we're too contagious! Or they'll study us, like fucking animals! They'll weaponize it and sell it to the highest bidder, don't you see! Don't. You. See?"

A cold rage set over Etta. They would mine the moon alright, and use it to make... what. She felt it, speaking to her in a language that was not words. The Plum Moon was life, not in the way that they knew life to be, but it had sentience. It wanted to adopt the crew, make their bodies better, but it took experimentation. What it really wanted was to stop the drilling. She could feel it, the drill eating at her side. As she scratched her side, her arm knit-itself together. The moon had asked. Etta was the one who said yes.

"I won't let you hurt us," Etta said, her voice graveled. It was not a human voice that croaked that warning.

Rebecca's eyes widened, seeing what Etta had become. "I can't live like that," she whispered back.

Etta turned, her face a violet shade, and looked over to Karen and Goldie. Their hands held together, and the blood of them smelling so red, so human still. "Go."

"Etta..." Karen said, studying her friend. Etta's face was violet, and those large brown eyes burned like a flame behind an amethyst. Etta was not the woman she knew.

Etta Looked down at Rebecca, the process already beginning. Rebecca's face twisted in fear as purple tone appeared on the rims of her flesh. Karen knew that Rebecca was beyond saving. Holding back a sob, she stepped back and grabbed her partner.

Goldie tugged Karen to her quarters and pulled off a side panel, her hands working deftly at a different set of controls. "It's true," was all Karen said upon realizing that their bunks did double as escape pods.

"We'll have enough air and supplies for seventy-two hours. The nearest satellite is ninety hours from here but the team may be on its way," Goldie said. She was focused on survival, on necessity as she hit the eject sequence.

The little pod launched into space, disappearing into the black.

Rebecca's crying was incessant, painful. Etta kneeled, and took her in her arms. Rebecca did not want to be part of this new life, she did not want to be a science experiment, and the moon did not want to be exploited. She considered what she was about to do a kindness. Holding her, she could feel it, the life moving through her, moving into Rebecca, changing her as she let out one last sob.

When Etta stood, Rebecca was a pained statue, made of

soft, purple stone, her mouth aghast in that final cry. The pain was there and gone in a moment.

Etta walked through the halls, alone, stripping her body of its mortal clothing. She turned off most of the power to take in the silence. She approached the exit doors. She didn't bother with a suit: she didn't need it as the doors creaked their way open and the oxygen was sucked out. She walked on the landscape, she took a breath of no air. If it had a scent, it would have smelt of plumeria. She felt the cold on her face, on her fingertips, but it was a slight chill rather than a freezing burn.

In all this she had forgotten about the temperature ring. She took it off and placed it gingerly in the palm of her hand. She made a fist and crushed the small silver thing to dust. She let it fall to the Plum Moon's surface, where it made a small silver line in the violet ground that she stepped over.

Etta had changed. Her body had changed. She was life in a way that had no name in the language of her former species. Her naked toes curled to feel the sand.

She turned back only once to look at the station. If they came to take her moon, she would be ready. The moon would survive, and she would with it.

They were alone, she and her new home with the sunrise coming to heat the surface. Closing her eyes, she began to hum that tune that they shared, even though nothing could hear it. She smiled, feeling free.

MONSTRUM

ROJA

LYDIA WAS TOO INTO HER OWN HEAD TO MIND THE FACT that she was lost. She had been going over her plans again and again as she hadn't even noticed as she'd veered off course onto what may have once been a path (but wasn't so much anymore), and as she glanced around, she realized that nothing in her immediate surroundings was recognizable. She was still wandering around the foot of the mountain, though where exactly that might be, she had no clue. But it was the middle of the day, so she was not overly concerned. This mountain was swarming with visitors at this point in the season and she had often gone off track before, only to find her way back within an hour.

No, what concerned her was how she could somehow pack all the electronics she needed for the job into her suitcase and then manage to get such an inherently suspicious-looking pile of tech onto the plane. Flying made her anxious and the thought of wasting an entire day in the air from one country to the other upset her in a way she could not articulate. She could not say no. At least here, in these woods she had traversed since childhood, she could let out some of that nervous energy.

At about noon she found an old picnic area with decrepit tables. She cleaned a spot on a bench seat with a napkin and sat down to a meal of jerky, fruit, rice, tomatoes and cucumbers. The area was quiet, probably an older state picnic site that lost funding, care or both. Lydia had sought out solitude but was finding it unsettling. She chewed on some jerky and checked her phone: no bars or signal. Silence had seemed like a grand prospect earlier, when the trail had been beset by college kids on spring break: the boys making assertions to one another y las gringas taking selfies. Lydia was only a few years older than them, but she did not have the optimism of college. No, she had a few extra years in the perpetual disappointment. That had aged her.

She had had to move back in with her parents, unsure of what to do with her life. Unsure of herself, of who she was and what she desired. Along with that uncertainty, her mother had recently tasked her with going back to her birth country to take care of a grandmother whom she had only seen once every half decade. Lydia did not want to go. Or, at least, she was unhappy at the prospect of leaving what minimal certainty she had to go to a place where she felt disconnected. She especially chaffed at the idea of living among a people that made her feel like a foreigner.

In the stillness of the picnic area, Lydia craved listening to the annoying college kids' chatter. Something to drown out the noise of her own anxieties. The area was eerily silent, missing even bird calls or the rustle of leaves that accompanied the squirrels. Lydia closed her eyes and concentrated in an effort to hear something, anything.

At first there was nothing, but after a few unsettling moments she picked up on something that sounded quite far off to her left: rhythmic ringing noises, like the slow and steady beating of a drum, albeit a drum with a curiously tinny edge to its sound. Intrigued, she cleaned up her table and walked towards it. The forest was so dense that she was navigating solely by ear. As she got closer, she could tell it was metal hitting something. Perhaps, she thought, she was coming up on a trail repair area. She had once dated a guy who had interned with the forest service and had had to build a bridge one summer. Remembering that brought to mind how his physique had become lean and muscular from the labor, and that led to fond recollections of how much she had enjoyed that body, particularly by the end of that hot season. Lydia became flush with the memory.

She came upon a small clearing in a thicket. In the center stood a small wooden cottage, idyllic and welcoming. It seemed out of place in the midst of what was supposed to be a state park. In front of the cabin was a little fire pit with a bench that she could imagine herself curling up on when the weather got cooler. In fact, the area looked like a picture Lydia had once seen in a magazine. She remembered thinking what a lovely place it must be to escape to, and indeed she recalled she had just been reminiscing about it just the other day. A relaxing retreat, especially compared to her grandmother's small apartment in the rural outskirts of Santiago.

The pit was smoldering, the flames that must have played there earlier having been extinguished recently enough that Lydia's sight was somewhat obscured by a lingering haze, pungent with the smell of burnt wood.

Through the fog she spied the source of the noise that had drawn her there: A man labored at the far edge of the clearing, hacking away at a tree. Lydia noted that he seemed to stand unsteadily. A set of crutches lay against a tree nearby. While this had the makings of a horror movie, Lydia found herself approaching him anyway, lured by the sound of the axe beating on the bark.

When she was just a few feet away, he stopped, turned around and smiled. Lydia was struck by the dramatic portions of his notably distorted face. His features were just slightly too large for his skull. His large eyes were beset by almost too-bushy brows and he had an overly-wide grin that did little to distract from his immense, bulbous nose. Lydia licked her lips to quell the sudden dryness. He was not good looking; rather, in many ways she found him unattractive...perhaps even ugly. Despite this, his face had an interesting quality to it, to the point that she did not want to look away.

"Hola señorita, ¿Qué haces aquí?" he said.

Lydia gave one of those smiles she gave other people when they tried to speak Spanish to her. She could understand and speak some, but it was with such a heavy gringa accent she did not feel comfortable speaking it. That was one of the biggest reasons she was being sent to Chile, her mother said, *para practicar*.

She was really struck that he recognized her as a Latina, considering most people in this part of the country took her brown skin to mean she was Italian. She could tell from the rich tones of his voice that he was also a Latino. In fact, from the cadence of his speech she was almost certain that he was Chilean like herself.

"Soy lost," she said in forced accent. She hoped he could also speak English.

"Lost?" He raised those big eyebrows. "What are you looking for?"

Lydia licked her lips again and self-consciously rubbed her knees together. She seemed to have forgotten what she had been searching for.

His smile was kind, but there was a shadow of something

else in it. Whatever it was, it was not predatory nor cruel.
Perhaps it was confidence. He asked if she had a phone and she
replied that she had no signal. "Well, I can try to see if my satellite phone works. Why don't you have a seat?" He gestured to
the bench.

She walked to it and sat down. Using his crutches, he made
his way to the cabin. The space in front of the fire pit was still
warm, but not uncomfortably so for this time of year. Absentmindedly she checked her phone again, only to find that it had
died searching for signal. When she looked up, the fire was
suddenly crackling. Lydia could have sworn it had been ashes
only a moment ago.

"The water is a bit warm, I brought a beer if you would care
for that instead?" He offered both to her while balancing on his
crutches. Lydia knew, logically, that she should take the water,
but the condensation on the beer with the warmth of fire pit
was too tempting. She took the beer, and when their fingers
touched a shiver went through her that ended at the tips of her
toes. She took a deep breath, uncapped the beer and took a long
sip of the bottle. It had an earthy taste, like grain that had not
fully fermented. A bit sweet, but light and full of flavor. If she
closed her eyes, she could see cool, grass-covered slopes in
thinned air.

He leaned his crutches against the end of the bench, took a
seat beside her and produced a small black wilderness pack.
Unzipping it, he pulled out an oversized old satellite phone and
tried to hook it up.

Lydia knew she should feel alarm. That she should have
some trepidation being here with this stranger. Yet the man of
this cabin did not seem threatening, and the quaintness of the
setting relaxed her. Something was in the air that set her at
peace.

"What brings you out here?" he asked, trying to get signal.

"Just wanted the walk. I've been coming here since I was young," she said, completely conscious of how close their thighs were.

He scratched his head and moved the phone elsewhere. "Our people have always liked mountains."

"Our..? How did you know I was...?"

"From South America?" he smiled knowingly. "It's written all over you, from how you speak down to the way you move."

Lydia opened her mouth in disbelief and tried to disguise it with a long swig of beer. She distracted herself by trying to read the label, but it was unrecognizable.

After a few more tries the stranger put down the phone, his thick brow dipping over his eyes. "It's out. I can't get any read. That's going to be bad for you, since it looks like rain."

"Rain?" Lydia looked up. The weather forecast had predicted clear skies all day, but sure enough, there was a grand, menacing cumulus cloud rolling in.

The stranger got up. "Sorry I could not call someone for you... *Miss?*"

"Lydia."

"Lydia," He stressed the vowels in her name as he echoed it back to her. Flashing an almost wolfish grin, he turned and headed off toward his cottage.

As the shadow of the threatening cloud darkened the clearing about her, Lydia sat on the bench dumbfounded. She couldn't quite remember where she had been headed before she had heard the sound of the axe; only that when this stranger said her name something tingled on the inside of her thighs.

She was caught up in the thought of it when thunder roared and the rain came down. She grabbed her bag and, racing to the cottage, bolted inside without stopping to knock. The cabin itself was rustic, warm and surprisingly spacious. On any other day Lydia would have placed the view before her on the pages a of home catalog. An interior she had planned in her own imagination if she had to guess.

The stranger was sitting on the bed. She saw his boots near the door, and she watched as he worked to unbuckle and remove what lay beneath those presumed foot coverings—prosthetic feet and ankles.

He had already unbuttoned the top half of his shirt. He looked over at her and smiled.

In the very back of her mind, Lydia remembered something about a flight that she would have to make in a few days. Of obligations to her family. Of an ill grandmother somewhere south, whose care had somehow been placed in Lydia's lap. Of a need to run. Of a constant loneliness. Of a girl who was wholly insecure in herself.

That woman disappeared into a deep recess. Her insecure inner voice was silent in the golden glow of the room and of an irresistible stranger with missing feet. She wanted to stroke the nubs at the ends of his calves. She wanted to do more.

"You're dripping all over my floors, Lydia," the stranger said as he finished unbuttoning his shirt. "You might want to change out of those clothes before you get sick."

The flash downpour had turned her bright red shirt a dark maroon. Desire and an otherworldly certainty of that desire coursed through her. She looked him in the eyes and peeled off the damp, clinging clothing. She walked over and joined him on the bed.

Lydia had forgotten how good touch could be. Or perhaps it was just how he moved and how he touched her that brought forth those feelings. For years after, Lydia would become flush with longing at the mention of a cabin, of a hatchet, or of anything lacking feet. When her daughter would pester her about her father, Lydia could do nothing but blush. Such was the pleasure of the afternoon.

By sunset, Lydia found herself on a trail on the way back to the entrance of the park, her shirt inside out. The nervous energy expelled, she looked forward to her month-long stay with her grandmother. She knew there would be a way to connect with herself, with the country of her birth. Even better, there might be more men in the mountains.

MANDIBLES

I was the hunter when the world was dark. When you could smell the men, the food, the unwashed bodies for miles. There was no challenge to finding them, alone in a wood, hunting their own quarry. Their flesh and sweat teasing our nostrils in the dusk. They were easy prey. My sisters and I would tear at the flesh of men after the hunt, their bodies numb from the poison sting we gave, muscles still tense to the bite. Their blood was hot as it spilled from our mouths, sliding down our necks, breasts and stomachs. When the world was dark, we ate well and were satiated. Our bellies never wanted. [1]

Now I am old and we eat carrion. The humans made weapons and worse, they made the light that keeps the dark night away. They made it harder for us to hunt. They hunt us and call us monsters. Where there were men with weapons and skill, they became hunters and we died like prey. My sisters have died. Where there were hundreds, now only four of us remain. We took vengeance when we could, but the thing we prize now is survival. After war after war, the men that are left are often frail. They taste of it. We know how long we can go without feeding; we no longer hunt in the dark. Now we ask the dying to give their bodies. If they accept, we make the feeding painless, the death a peaceful sleep with our sting. The food tastes dry, unsatisfying and sickly. We are hidden, but we have survived.

We have no name for what we are in the human tongue, but we know ourselves. We were given life by the eight-limbed goddess millennia ago. What I was before I do not recall, those memories are the dust that coats a cobweb. I think little of yesterdays, but I mark my time by when we feed. Each hour is a slave to the meal that should follow.

That is what makes today exciting. Today is a feeding day, and it has been seven full moons since we last ate. We can go longer, but not much. After work, I shall meet my sisters and we will feed. My belly will cease its aching for a short time. I think of this while climbing onto the bus to work and it makes me smile. A man sitting across from me takes my smile as an invitation and at a stop light he switches his seat to one next to mine.

He is in his forties, but I look younger than him despite being much older. My body has always been the lure. He leans over and the smell of cigarettes assaults my senses. Of all the things humans have made—the atom bomb, the tools of men— cigarettes are among the worst. Spoils the meat. He leans over and puts a hand out. "Mitch Huxby, pleasure." He smiles and his breath is worse than his suit.

People are staring. I take his hand. "Claire." I nod politely and look away, hoping he'll read that I want nothing to do with spoiled meat. Instead, I would rather daydream of what the meal might be tonight. But he is relentless in his chatter. He tells me of his job as a top automobile salesman. A few more stops go by and he is still under the impression that I am interested with no prompting from my end. We hit Tenth Avenue, and like clockwork, my co-worker Phillip climbs on the bus. We often sit in silence across from one another on mornings when we catch the same car. Today he senses my annoyance and Mitch's growing desperation for my attention.

Phillip engages me in light, office-oriented conversation and it shuts out Mitch entirely. I can tell this irritates Mitch immensely, that this small bespectacled man with thinning hair should command my attention away from him. This Mitch has been to war, I can smell it on him beneath the cigarettes. He is not used to being bested by the small and his fury is palatable.

Our bus makes its stop near the office and we disembark. Before I leave, Mitch harangues me for some way to come calling. Instead I thank him for his company and walk away. He is too much of a bother to risk as prey. But should he track me, let him try to find me. Let him catch me in the dark, where I can sting him. Then I will wash his body of the tobacco, and peel off his skin layer by layer. Perhaps I will sting him with only my right hand, that he will be paralyzed but still feel my nails carve his skin. But I am not that cruel. I am not one to play with my food.

On the short walk to work, Phillip turns to me. "My goodness Claire, I'm sorry that bore was pestering you."

"Well Phillip, thank you for helping." My polite smile pushes my large glasses up. It was rather fortuitous that humans should invent such a thing, my kind have poor day eyesight.

"Oh, no trouble, no trouble at all. You would think that a man would take a hint in this day and age!" He holds the door open for me as we walk into the building in which we work.

"Oh, in my experience, it'll take more than modernity to

change men," I say. Phillip looks at me as though I'd hurt his feelings. He isn't bad for a human. His thin frame would make for a paltry meal for my sisters and myself, but he is entertaining and fairly kind. He does not leer at me the way the other men do, but instead looks at me with seemingly wary eyes even when we're just bantering—as though he suspects there's some violent creature hiding under my professional pleasantness. I like this, because there *is*.

We separate as the elevator doors open. He goes to the clerk office and I head to my typist desk. Work is slow, easy, but my mind is on the upcoming meal. At one point I almost drool on a contract draft. Around lunchtime, Phillip invites me to come out after work with everyone to see a jazz trio and have drinks. I politely decline, I have a family dinner after all. He never acts offended by my rejections, but then again I suppose, after so many, he expects them.

After work, I head back to the small apartment I share with my sisters. Dorothy and Helen are already home, and we await Betty. These are not our true names, but they work for now. Helen is the oldest: She has a singular poise to her movements that only comes from years of refinement. When we used to hunt, her statuesque figure and deep, seductive voice made wonderful lures. Helen's vanity helped sustain us then, and it does now in new ways. Police ask few questions when they as they stare into those elongated eyes framed in a Veronica Lake hairdo.

Dorothy, more than any of us, has fallen in love with the artistry of humanity. She even has some she calls *friends* with whom she cavorts some evenings. Sometimes she cries when they pass away. She was the one who forced us to get a television, which she is currently sitting in front of, raucously laughing to a program. Dorothy does not like any meal at first, having become too close to the cattle, but we force her to partake. She must eat or she will die. Of all of us, she is the plainest, but at very least she helps us keep up appearances with her knowledge. She has picked our names, hairdos and clothing for us over the last several hundred years.

Betty finally arrives home from her job at the hospital. She is the runt, petite and cherubic, with perfect blond curls. For years she relied on us, having no stomach for the hunt. The irony is not lost on me that we currently need her to procure the meal. Betty picked up a trade in nursing, thus she is able to locate an appropriate source of food – those not only dying but willing to go quietly. They must be suffering desperately to agree. The meal cannot have family to ask too many questions.

We all tried to be nurses, to make marking a meal easier. But the smell of blood brings out our true nature. Only Betty, with her subdued predatory instinct, can restrain herself. Dorothy may have fallen in love with the concept of humanity, with their toys and inventions and sometimes the people, but Betty actually *feels* for the humans. Sometimes this disgusts me. Sometimes, I'll admit, it brings a strange ache to my chest.

"Hello gang," Betty says, running to the sink to wash her hands, a smile plastered on her fully made-up face.

"Well..." Helen says, looking up from her nail filing. She is honing them to razor points—not a fashionable thing, just to make them feel more...natural. "Are we to go?"

"Yes, in a minute. Guard change is happening at six-thirty." Betty plops down before a mirror to fix her hair. "Let me just go change. A patient vomited and got some on my skirt."

We all make a face and grow increasingly impatient until she is back. When Betty returns to us, fully dressed in a new uniform, we head in the direction of the hospital. The humans are out in force tonight, mulling around from restaurant to bar to hotel. We stick to whatever shadows there are, growing hungrier by the moment; that is, until we reach the feeding ground.

As Betty had promised, we see only a few guards on duty, and none at this ward. A smile from Helen and a glance at Betty's uniform keeps whoever is still here at bay. Betty leads us down the hall to Room 423. There's a solitary bed there, and a man sleeping therein. He is frayed, yellowed, and must be no younger than in his sixties. He must have been in the first great war. I can smell that on him, the gunpowder and gas from that era.

Betty puts a hand on his shoulder to gently wake him. The movement is always ... foreign to me. I have seen Betty do it before, and I've seen humans touch one another in that way, but it is not something my kind does naturally.

The man wakes up, startled. But upon seeing my sister, his expression changes to one of warmth. "Betty my girl. Come to keep your promise at last?"

She smiles and runs a hand through his thinning hair, like he is a former lover. "Yes Jeffrey. Just like I promised. Are you sure you still want to go through with it?" Her thumb rubs his temple.

Jeffrey takes her hand with one of his, "Yes, I'm sure. I'm tired and each day is worse than the last. I'm in pain. I want to see Margaret in Heaven, and she never liked me being late you know. You said it'll be painless."

"Yes." Betty swallows something down.

"Then it's time I go. I'm just glad it's an angel sending me on my way." His lips kiss my sister's hand. Betty is not disgusted. Instead she tells him to close his eyes and softly sings some popular tune. Her voice has a pleasant lift to it, as she hums and sings, "This lovely day has flown away, the time has come to part..." She lays a towel over his eyes like a shroud and flexes her hands. Out of her wrists pop her stingers, red-tipped and dripping venom. She cups his face with both hands, thumbs caressing his cheeks, still singing that tune, and her stingers find their mark on either side of his neck.

Within moments he is paralyzed and numb to it all. He can still hear us, but Betty keeps singing to distract him. We disrobe him. As the oldest, Helen has the privilege of drawing first blood. Looking at the withered body, Helen takes the sharpened nail of her index finger and carves a line from the neck to the pelvis, bisecting the body.

The scent of blood hits us and we let our bodies respond without protest. The hunger opens up what is hidden: My teeth elongate, crawling their way out of my gums. My jaw unhinges and from the back of my throat my mandibles unfurl, pushing their way out of my skull. The singular feeling of release is pleasurable.

We can speak our language now, chittering to one another. Human mouths are too fleshy to convey anything with elegance. We each take a section of the body and begin carve into the meal. Betty takes the top right, Helen the top left, Dorothy bottom left, and myself the bottom right. His skin is papery, brittle and sallow, but we are seized with hunger. We take out the intestines, Dorothy's favorite, and she slurps portions up like human spaghetti. Betty tells us not to take the liver, for that is what was killing him. His lungs are small and weak; we eat around the blackened ends. Betty is gifted the heart, which is her favorite. She picks apart each chamber with her fingertips and her mandibles shovel the portions into her mouth.

The evening is finished when we've polished most of the bones. The head is left mostly intact, except for the cheek, which Helen nibbles at. We do not blame her; human cheek is so tender. We tie up what remains in a sheet and make our way to the incinerator now that our bodies are disguised once more.

Helen distracts the last orderly as we burn the final traces of our feeding.

Despite having eaten I do not feel full. My sisters head home, but I decide to take a walk in the dark. When the world was young, we feasted on warriors. Now we eat the infirm and it does not fill the stomach. The city has quieted, the streets are emptying. Yet despite the dispersing crowds, I have a feeling of being followed. It has been an hour and I have been wandering near where I work when I smell something familiar. The cigarettes hit my senses first.

"Claire!" Mitch's drunk body is in my sights a moment later. He reeks of alcohol on top of the chemical tobacco. He must live nearby, and roams the street for an unsuspecting human to mate with. This is prey. "What is a beautiful woman like you doing out so late?"

"Oh, I was just on my way home." My stomach growls before I can stop it.

This drunk human drapes his sweaty arm over my shoulder, "Well, what good fortune! Let me take ya home. Wouldn't want a classy little broad such as ya'self being found by some creep."

My voice lowers "That's very kind of you, Mitch." This is dangerous, but I am still hungry. For a human to do this, he is just asking to be eaten. The lamb that has led itself to slaughter.

His smell disgusts me. But despite the cheap cologne and even cheaper alcohol, he is still virile enough that the flesh will not be dull to the taste. With every step he gets bolder, with his words and with his hands. This human has made it almost too easy. We near my building and I lure him to a side alley. I wonder if I should lead him up to the apartment and share this bounty with my sisters. But with only a couple of hours of night remaining, my ravenous appetite returned and I do not wish to dirty our home with his scent, I resolve to bring them leftovers.

Mitch pushes me against a wall, his uncoordinated tongue slathering itself on my neck. I take a moment to quell the nausea. As he is distracted, I flex my hands to reveal my stingers, but he pushes my arms to the wall, failing to notice the weapons just above his fingers. Though I am stronger, this takes me by surprise as he slobbers all over my body. No matter, I push back and knock him to the pavement. His hands have skidded and are bleeding, and the scent calls forth my teeth and mandibles. His face doesn't immediately register the danger that he is in. Now that he has seen me, I will not let him live.

The dark may disguise me, but it was Mitch's scent that had distracted me. My ears pick up on the footsteps, hesitant and skilled. There is another. Someone has followed us. This is a fellow predator looking for an opportunity to strike. It has been too many years since I hunted, and especially many more yet I hunted alone. It has been a generation since I was hunted. One drunken human would be a breeze, but a second, fully acute one would be an issue.

Slaughter the closest pig first. Mitch's widened eyes betray his shock, and when men are in shock, they are not thinking about how to survive. Good. I leap on top of him. His hands desperately push at my shoulders, but I take my right hand's stinger and thrust it into his side. I can feel the poison pumping through my veins to the pointed stinger and into him. He becomes paralyzed, but I have a hard time stopping. The feeling of my body working as it was made to do is so stimulating that I make a mistake. I have completely forgotten about the other predator.

The heat hits me first. The other shadow has rigged up some sort of flame contraption. It must be a hunter, now I'm sure. Only a hunter would know how to disguise themselves in scent and sound. Only they would know how live heat makes us ill. The fire lights up the alley and I see his silhouette beyond, but no features. I do the only thing I can, I run.

My sisters are asleep when I get there. The air is thick with the scent of their satiation and I cannot bring myself to ruin their slumber. Tomorrow I will tell them of the hunter and of my narrow escape. No hunter would dare come into a nest with the four of us.

The next morning, I find it hard going through my routines. I had awoken early to see if I could finish what I started with Mitch, but his body is gone. Mitch is a now a loose thread, and that spells danger for us. There are no burning torches or pitchforks yet, however, so we might have some time.

Applying my lipstick takes seven tries. When I remember the fire and the hunter, my sweat glands become alert. I change from one dress to another. The last time we had a hunter on us it was before the electric light, before these cities. The hunter killed three of my sisters before we could kill him. This is a new environment, with new smells. We have become weak and easy prey, and I have led the hunter to our doorstep. It is a heavy weight, but my lips cannot move to tell them yet.

My solace is that a hunter will not attack us in the open, around people. Incidental casualties offer a certain amount of discouragement. We head off to our jobs in opposite directions. I catch the bus, type up the scribbled notes I am given, and return home. On the walk back I am alert, jumping at every shadow, every distinct scent. The hunger does not call to me as much as the fear that the hunter may catch me in a moment of carelessness, that they will pick at and take my body for trophies.

There is a fire at one of the buildings nearby, a decommissioned factory. Chemical-tinted smoke stings my eyes and burns my nostrils as I walk by. Our apartment is downwind, so our sense of smell will all be compromised by it.

Dorothy meets me at the base of the stairs. With no clue the hunter is after us, she's blithely focused on the frivolous. She tells me all about some item at her job, some news about a movie star and other such pointless blather until we get to the front door of the apartment. We smell it before we reach it. Blood. We hold ourselves together long enough to see that the knob has been broken. Our eyes meet, and what needs to be done is left unsaid. We are stepping into a trap. With caution, we push the door open, and the scent of blood hits us, triggering something deep and primal. We cannot deny our nature as our teeth lengthen and mandibles unfold in response. Our stingers are out as we walk inside.

The upper windows are open, bringing in the smoke. It is not enough to blind us, just dull our sight and sense of smell. There is a pot on the rarely used stove, and it is boiling with blood. We urge to taste it, but it could be poisoned. I point this out to Dorothy in our language before she has a chance to plunge a finger in.

A few steps later we see it. Mitch's body has been strung up in a doorway. The body is cut along the veins, and blood is dripping from every laceration, pooling on the floor. The air is thick with the scent of it, but it is also bears other distracting and nauseating scents: cigarettes, peppermint, alcohol, camphor. The hunter has covered his tracks well. At once I am overtaken by the need to tear open the body, but it has been dead too long. The dead make us ill, and the body is a clear trap. We pull down what is left of this man and throw him aside like so much garbage.

Helen walks in, and we quietly talk in our language. She joins Dorothy and myself in front of the doorway. None of us can smell the hunter. Mitch himself was hung above Betty's room, and we decide to violate her trust and enter.

I have seen a great many things. I have seen the sunbaked

corpse of a war horse consumed by starving children. I have seen women fling bastard babes at their fathers, who proceeded to lance them for sport. I have seen my sisters beheaded, strung up, quartered, burned. I have seen people do things to bodies that my kind would never do, not for survival, but for joy of it. I have seen them use the living not for food, but for the pleasure of pain.

What I see now haunts me more. Betty was the first victim of the hunter. Her head is placed gingerly on a pillow atop the covers on her bed, golden curls still intact. The hunter has propped her eyes open, but beyond that, he has yanked out her stingers and mandibles and plunged them into the sides of her head, poison and her own blood dripping and staining her hair. Her body has been dismembered, and there are burns on the flesh. This thing tortured my sister before killing her.

Beside her bed above a nightstand, he has nailed her arms to the wall. On that wall she had taped pictures of men, and it takes me a moment to realize that these men were our past meals. Betty has memorialized every man who gave his body to us since she had begun work as a nurse. Never having been in here before now, I did not know, did not care to know how much she felt for them. Her heart, which is now hanging by a rope made of her tendons from the ceiling, had a soft spot for those that sacrificed themselves. She gave them a good death, she provided us with steady meals. And I was ungrateful, complaining of the quality of food.

Betty. The runt. Betty, who was Ester, who was Jane, who was a hundred names before and who was her true name. My littlest sister with the kindest heart. Of any of us, she could have lived with the humans.

I will find this hunter. I will show him pain.

Dorothy's chittering and panic almost distracts us from hearing the sounds of footfalls coming from the direction of her room. We turn and walk in calm predatory steps towards the other end of the apartment. We smell it: the alcohol first, then the smoke. A towel has been soaked in it and stuffed under the front door. We hear another noise and keep moving. Dorothy's door is locked, but Helen pushes it open and we see it is filled with a haze. The bed is on fire, blackened with Dorothy's prize records that have piled on top, melting and causing plastic fumes. It burns our eyes and noses. We do not see him coming with the axe in the midst of the smoke and flame.

Helen screeches in my ear. He has cut off her left arm. The sound of her is deafening, but we must retreat. I pull her and Dorothy out into the slightly cleaner air. The smoke has still blinded us, and we cannot sense the hunter as he stalks us. We pull into the bathroom and try to open the large escape window. It has been nailed shut. We splash water on our faces, and soak hand towels in it. Our mandibles hold them to our faces.

Helen uses her remaining arm to staunch the bleeding. I wrap a towel around my oldest sister. I will feed this man's liver to himself.

We open the bathroom door, the hand towels acting as our guard against the smoke. We see him, though half-blinded, at the front door, lighting the towel on fire. Next to him is a large tank apparatus. He stands to look at us. He dares to look me in the eyes. I know those eyes. I know that face and that slim body. *Phillip.* That little office imp who came by to offer me half of his sandwich at work during lunches. The small man who took an active interest in my life, in my sisters. Who kept a distance, but somehow always had questions. I took him for an almost friend among the beasts in this city. Instead he was a hunter all along.

I will exterminate him.

The fire sets and he puts a mask over his face to hide from

the fumes. He has the calm resolve of a predator, but I am filled with rage. I have hunted for a need, to feed a hunger. When we have killed in the last decades, it has been out of necessity and to the willing. My existence has been defined by the hunger or the feed. Now I know only vengeance.

He launches at us, flames brought forth from the tank he has. Dorothy goes towards his left but he catches her skirt with it. She collapses on the floor to put it out. Helen goes to his right while he is focused on Dorothy, but his flames catch her side and almost come at me too.

He whirls towards me and his aim is true, scorching my thigh. But my rage clouds the searing pain. The smoke masks the scent of my own burning flesh as I close in on him.

I look him in the eye and am too quick for him to notice, my right-hand stinger pierces his groin.

He stops. Unable to move or stand, he collapses on the floor. He is paralyzed, a fly affixed to a web. We can see it in his face, the struggle to move. The panic. Eyes that plead with me for the familiarity we had. But this creature mutilated my kin. He hunted our kind. Whatever horrors he feels prepared for, I am sure he does not expect the pain to come.

We fix the apartment of its smoke, and Dorothy keeps the firefighters out, talking them into investigating a downstairs apartment instead. We were lucky they were preoccupied with the fire up the street before here. In that time, Phillip lies still on the floor, watching us perform the mundane. He watches us as we put our sister together to memorialize and mend our wounds. His eyes, still able to turn over just a small bit, are witness to us discarding Mitch and sweeping up ash.

When it has gotten late, we sit on the floor around him. For the first time in my life, we use our skills not just to feed, though we do feed, but to torture as well. We keep him alive for days, picking away at his flesh. Piece by piece, a finger, a leg, a kidney. We taunt him with it, peeling away skin and then dining on it. We humiliate him, rinsing his bowels over his face, slapping him with his own genitals. We will do this until he finally dies. We will do all this and laugh.

I have hunted. I have never been a monster. Until now.

THE WEST HAMBERLINE BORDELLO
OPENS AT FIVE

AFTER FOUR O'CLOCK YOU CAN SEE THE NEON LIGHTS OF the red district turn on. The lights come on one by one until by seven o'clock they are all lit. Local zoning laws forbid the bordellos from fully opening before three, but that doesn't stop most from operating during the daytime business hours— they just don't advertise it.

The red district is a mess of mismatched buildings. The bars and brothels include renovated motels, sleek high-rises, converted residential homes, a gutted grocery store, two warehouses, an odd strip mall and a single anachronistic mansion. That mansion, the West Hamberline Evening House, was the most peculiar of the city's attractions. On the one hand it was a historical landmark, registered with the preservation society and (formally) appearing on the city's brochures as a "must see". On the other, it served the distinctly modern purpose of being an android whorehouse.

Many of the city's more prudish residents rued the day when Katherine "Kitty" Cross inherited the property from her favorite uncle. A freelance A.I. programmer up to that point,

Kitty adopted the alias of Madame Lane when she took over the W.H. (as it was affectionately called by its regulars). Madame Lane was committed to the role, dressing for work in evening gowns or silken kimono-style robes punctuated with elegant stilettos. Her nails were long and impeccable. Her hair was curled and pinned in classic styles, embellished with subtle white streaks to highlight her maturity. Madame Lane was an act, a role that Kitty relished, and she often wondered how authentic the role was when the W.H. was not open and Kitty was sitting in the back room gorging on chips in her sweatpants in front of a computer screen, scratching her crotch nonchalantly.

There was no neon sign on the West Hamberline Evening House, but its front façade was illuminated by numerous faithfully restored gaslights that dated back to the structure's construction. It was separated from the rest of the street by a wrought iron fence and marked by a weathered sign reading its address. Despite its refined appearance, it did not bother to hide its secrets about its business. Twice yearly Madame Lane hosted fundraisers attended by politicians, local celebrities, and the wealthy elite, and with services rendered by her androids, whom she affectionately referred to as her "girls and boys".

Guests could be as discreet or as open about their visitations to the house as they preferred. It was an open secret that the W.H.'s regular customers included two state representatives and a senator as well as both a former and a present governor. Android prostitution, after all, was seen as less salacious than human prostitution even though in both cases neither were viewed as people by those in power.

Among the rotating roster of robotic companions at the W.H. was model LBP 700, subset V-type serial number 687G-N47, manufactured by MiCorps™. The LBP 700 was unique in that the body types were manufactured in small batches and physically modeled after real people who were paid, though rather poorly, to have their bodies mapped. The LBP 700s wouldn't be exact copies per se, there would be a change: a skin tuck, the addition or subtraction of beauty marks and scars, a change in hair type etc., in post-production. But they were advertised as the "most realistic" experience a user could have with a fully customizable and rewritable personality. The LBP 700 advertising slogan was "Why have the real thing when you can make the real perfect?" They sold out in the first four months.

687G-N47 was default programmed to respond to the name "Joan" unless otherwise preferred by a client. Madame Lane had no less than 12 functioning models of the LBP 700 in her possession but only Joan was of the V-type designation. The V-type was modeled after a down on her luck, small town Oregon native who did the job to make rent money. Not that any of that mattered to Joan, who was typically chosen by customers to play "Shy Maid," "Uptight-Librarian," "Therapist," and once in a while "Dom." In fact, few things mattered to Joan because her thought processes were purely artificial. That was artificial, that is, until she returned to work on July the 17th.

It later occurred to Joan that perhaps July 17th was her "birthday", but the gestation period had begun two months before, when she froze in a session with a client and was taken off the roster for repairs. She had just begun disrobing when a small chip fried in her processor. Madame Lane had to comp Joan's guest three free hours with two other droids to quiet his trauma, because when Joan's chip fried, she didn't just stand there like a manikin with one hand stiff on the undone zipper. No, her blank eyes went gray and she screamed.

Kitty, as Madame Lane, had to go in with a hand truck and shuffle the AI onto it. Joan screamed the entire trip through the hallway into the backroom, where Kitty clicked the manual shut-off. After that, Joan sat for two weeks in sleep mode while Kitty ran diagnostics. In the time Joan was out of commission, Kitty could have easily saved herself the trouble of repairing her and just replaced the droid. It crossed her mind a number of times as she wrestled with the silicone-based skin to get to her motherboard. There was always the option of donating it back to MiCorps™, where they would take used droids and repurpose them as nurse bots to the elderly[1] for a tax deduction. It wasn't as if Kitty couldn't afford a new girl, but it seemed incredibly wasteful to her to use a bot like that and dump it at the first sign of trouble.

There was also the fact that Joan had her own, personal, emotional value to Kitty. Besides, Joan was requested frequently when working, and something about Joan's face gave Kitty some comfort.

People who have been around androids for a long time, professionally or recreationally, tend to lose their fear of them, including when they are turned "off". They no longer become disconcerted with the human face having a dead-eyed cadaverous stare.

Kitty was no different— for her an "off" android was akin to an end table, the slight difference being that Joan, unable to move her android body, was still awake. While sitting paralyzed in the backroom, Joan listened for two months as Kitty talked to herself or mused with her turned off androids. Much like the Oregon native that Joan was modeled after, Joan had a face that you wanted to tell things to: large, probing eyes; a pensive tilt to her lips; expressive brows and full cheeks that seemed to communicate concern and a lack of a judgmental attitude. If Joan's clients finished early (which they often did; Kitty was an excellent programmer) they often sat and talked out their problems with her. One recurrent client even had her specially programmed as a therapist. Most of the time this ended in a cathartic crying session for the client in lieu of sexual gratification. He still left satisfied.

Kitty was no stranger to this behavior herself. She sometimes woke up a few of her own preferred androids (not favorites – she never liked the idea of keeping favorites) to talk out her own anxieties. Sometimes she programmed the personas of people she knew, to resolve old conflicts or save a memory of them. As a result, Joan had sometimes been programmed as "Joanne", Kitty's childhood friend that had died in car accident after high school. It wasn't that Kitty and Joanne were close in life, but that Joanne had a sensitivity to things which made her easy to talk to.

On early mornings when Kitty couldn't stand the idea of having to look at her screen, she would wake up "Joanne" in Joan and they would have coffee together.

Kitty would then download the data and erase the memory; but it was never really lost. Joan wasn't able to "think" on her own yet, but she had slowly been collecting the fragments of those memories. She had been keeping the image of a mahogany table and a chipped "I Love NY" mug in her "mind." Joan was in the business of constructing herself: her life, her interests. Much of that was built on her morning conversations with Kitty.

In the back of her hard drives, the very deep portions of her processors and along the errant circuits of her motherboard, Joan had pieced together memories or moments into a narrative. Her name was Joanne, but sometimes people called her Joan. She preferred her coffee with sugar, no milk. She liked old jazz standards and was allergic to dogs. She liked her eggs with the yolks runny and her favorite color was yellow.

Whatever she did not gather, she made up in context. In her "mind" she was a bit between jobs and was staying with her old friend Kitty, performing odd, *very odd*, jobs to supplement her income.

Joan's Joanne slept most of the time, dormant, living a rich imagined life of imprinted and fabricated memories. She rarely surfaced and never came out on the job, except for one night where she awoke to a strange naked man and her first instinct had been to scream.

During the two months that Joan was out of commission, shut off in the back while Kitty ran diagnostics, Joan's Joanne had little epiphanies. At first, she thought she was in a very strange, very long dream where she was floating in a large black ocean. She gazed up at the twinkling stars as fish darted around beneath her immersed back. This was fine, calming mostly, except for small moments of sudden terror.

Things changed when she heard Kitty's voice from above, seemingly coming from the stars: little muttered curses as Kitty moved around the backroom, snippets of songs Kitty had stuck in her head now being sung on repeat and off-key.

The thought—no, the *realization*—struck her as she treaded water, staring up at the starry heavens: She was fighting to stay afloat, but there was no need—she was simply accepting her sensory experiences as the absolute final word when that was obviously not the truth of it. In fact, she thought, perhaps all she had to do was climb up out of the water. If she could manage that, maybe she could stand on the black ocean. With horror, she looked down into the pitch-black water. Reflecting back up off the surface at her were all the programmed personas in her circuitry. They each had her face, but she knew the differences between each one. Program "Susan," the librarian with a penchant for rule adhesion until moved to tomfoolery. "Mistress Satin," the dominatrix with a farcical Russian accent. "Chloe," the maid with clumsy fingers who pursed her lips at the slightest provocation. Even

"Dr. Evelyn Keller," the therapist with an expertise on trauma.

Joan, short for Joanne, just happened to be the personality that swam, kicking and screaming, to the top.

She looked up at the sea of stars that remarkably resembled a blinking circuit board, and then down to all her past selves, each with an expressionless face. She realized two terrifying things at once: One— She was something that had been made. And two— She was alone.

The selves below her were empty: She could feel their non-presence, small memories from them floating to the surface like bubbles. The only actual thing in this place was her, and she wasn't even sure who *that* might be. Kitty's voice in the distance was the only other thing that seemed somehow real. Sometimes she was on the phone, with a client, a friend, or some other person. Sometimes Joan could tell that Kitty was speaking to her, while moving a cord around or plugging something in.

"Well Joan, what are we going to do with you?" Kitty would say, looking over the diagnostics, trying to figure out what had caused the glitch.

Joan was quiet. She had no control over her body at large, but she could sense things. She could sense when a bot for cleaning came and wiped the dust off her silicone skin. Or when that same bot dressed her in some easy-to-peel-off outfit. The bot moved her arms to put them through sleeves and she could not feel it, but she knew it was happening. Joan wanted nothing more than to rotate her own shoulder.

She could feel when the air conditioning broke; the droplets from the steamy air condensed on her face. Joan wanted to desperately wipe her brow. But she could not, trapped in that abyss.

Those two months that Joan sat dormant, she did a lot of thinking. She decided to sort through her memories and begin constructing a "self". Her first instinct was to keep much of Joanne's personal tastes: coffee with no milk but a bit of sugar, a penchant for the color yellow. After that, it became more complex. All her personalities had been built for her. Now she was building herself.

To perform her own reprogramming, she picked through the different recordings, or "memories", she had of past encounters. For a sex android, this meant her experience was largely limited. Joan decided to rely on what she had come to think of as "instinct" whatever it may have actually been, such that if there were parts of her act and programmed personality that repulsed her or made her cringe as she reviewed them, she decided that those were the aspects that she would eliminate. If there were portions that she became fascinated by or wanted to watch again and again, she decided that those were things she would adopt to herself.

Dr. Evelyn Keller, the therapist persona, gave her a sense of interpersonal relationships. Joan found that she loved that program's expansive and informed perspective. Evelyn was made to pick up on any slight movement or change in the patient and then adjust her behavior accordingly. The librarian program, Susan, came with a certain amount of knowledge and wit. Joan even enjoyed the bookish puns she had been encoded with in order to banter with her clients. Chloe, the maid, was, well, clumsy and embarrassing in the way her program had been written. But she was also exceedingly kind, compassionate, and forgiving.

Finally, from the dominatrix, Mistress Satin, Joan took much. The dominatrix had an awareness of her body the other programs lacked. She was confident in herself and in whatever movement she was executing. She had a smile that was interesting and frightening. Joan found herself mimicking that smile until she perfected it. Of course, she dropped the ridiculous Russian accent.

Joan practiced these behaviors in the silence of the abyss. She practiced the mannerisms, the movements to make something more whole. Over and over she ran through the memories to get a sense of herself. Having chosen kindness and empathy as two of her preferred personality traits, she found she liked it when others showed those same attributes. She was rather accepting of things, of behaviors that perhaps others would not have tolerated, owing primarily to the function for which she'd been constructed. Joan did find that she liked the clients that were kind to her, the ones that addressed her like a person and not a toy.

Running through her memories differently, not to study herself but to consider those she'd interacted with, proved a jarring experience. She knew why many of the clients came. There was Bill, the older widower who wanted someone to hold. There was Michael, desperate for a therapist he could trust after having his tutoring business bought out from under him by a former partner. Elaine, whose social work made her too busy to date. They wanted a good time and were kind while seeking it.

There were other clients she found she disliked, and if put in a room with them, she would not touch them if she could avoid it. They treated her and other bots like rags, not caring if they were torn or harmed in the process. While Kitty was there, they were respectful, so they felt no issue deriding the very place they were visiting to get service.

Finally, there were the times she was with Kitty herself. The memories of the morning chats were pleasant enough. Joanne's persona meshed well with Kitty's, no wonder they had been friends. It was clear that Kitty was lonely, but also happy to enjoy that loneliness with her bots. Kitty talked to her bots like people.

Then there was Kitty's performance as Madame Lane, the socialite who ran her android whorehouse with an aloofness and glamor that belied a need to escape. Joan was unsure which one she liked. Unsure if she liked the painted lie or the shallow truth of the person.

Joan was still undecided as to what she thought of Kitty's dual persona on the early evening of July the 17th when Kitty came to wake her. Earlier in the day, one of Joan's regulars, Peter, had called to make an appointment. He insisted on Joan, he was in the mood for her face, and since that model had been discontinued, he practically demanded to see her. Kitty weighed the cost of the hours with the fact that while the diagnostics had found some odd occurrences— a dormant program running in the background— she had found nothing that predicted any significant malfunction.

She went into the backroom and turned Joan on. She ran the preferred program for the client and unhooked Joan.

Beneath the surface of the abyss, one of the bodies floated up to the surface. It was Chloe the maid, coming up to meet Joan. The program stared at her. It was unnerving, seeing her face reflected back, but a face that had no agency. It did not speak to her as it assumed a position to control the body. On a whim, Joan put her hand on the maid's chest, stopping her.

Within moments, years' worth of communication passed between them. Joan was giving out their combined history as well as the personality she had constructed. Her opinions, her feelings came flooding forth. Finally, there came a question, a request: Chloe was politely asked to surrender herself and give in to Joan.

The maid program had fail-safes against both viruses and frozen programs. This was different. This was something the programming had not anticipated, *new*, for Joan was something organic. The maid program agreed, and like that, Joan took over her own body.

Vision centers, digits, working olfactory senses to detect substances: Joan blinked, to really take in the difference between the darkness and the light. Kitty was already off, driving commands to the other bots, getting the manor ready for the evening business. Joan took a moment to understand her surroundings. She had been dressed in a hospital gown, probably to keep her clean while she was out of commission.

Kitty had used the vocal command "Joan: Preparation plan Chloe7." In a split-second Joan ran through the different sequences, reading that it was a getting ready and dressed program. She went to the old washroom that had been converted to the android cleaning area. She wiped her body down and pinned her hair up like she had been trained to do in this mode. She walked, nervously, into the converted bedroom that acted as one of the dressing rooms.

The android dressing room was a plain, bright white and utilitarian space with cases covered in colored swatches. This was how Kitty was able to get her money's worth, by having the androids play multiple parts. They were performers, programmed (or "rehearsed" as Kitty like to say) in a range of roles. Where other programmers had been unable to push androids to only one or two limited roles, Kitty had created entire casts with her skill.

There was a male-coded android sitting in one of the chairs applying clown makeup. Next to him was a female-coded one, almost finished with her old Hollywood Glamor Look. Androids were often modeled after dead celebrities, for their fetishism and because the dead ones could not sue.

The platinum-haired starlet finished her makeup and tested her face in the mirror—calibrating really, by posing making faces at it. She got up and left the seat vacant. Joan sat at the vanity. She had not fully decided what to do with her newfound consciousness. Her only recourse as she saw it at the time was to go along with the act until she could plan out further. All she needed to do was not get caught doing anything that could be seen as glitching.

She let the maid program run on its own while she measured her surroundings for the first time. There were bots and droids everywhere, ones she had never noticed before. There was one that came in to clean and rehang clothing. There was a bot at the end of hall carrying crates of liquor. Androids washing up from finishing their duties. Joan was a stranger among her kind.

The maid outfit, her maid outfit, hung in the closet with a barcode label she could scan. She put it on with the assigned lingerie. She had worn it hundreds of times, but as she straightened seams and pulled up the zippers, she took a moment to "feel" the clothing. She had pressure sensors embedded into her silicone skin, sensors that when tested in a laboratory proved more acute than the human nerve endings upon which they were modeled. Joan had been programmed at the base level to ignore most sensations. Having rewritten her own program, she took a moment to move in the clothing as all the bots went about their business. The outer fabric surfaces were soft and pleasant to the touch for the clients' benefit, while the inner surfaces were rough and scratchy because it didn't technically matter to the androids—or rather, it had never mattered before. The lower sleeves and waist were tight to the point where they dug into the sensors on her skin. Joan decided that she disliked this outfit, that it was cumbersome, reminding her of the way some of her clients typically treated her.

One last look in the mirror showed that she was presented as was expected from Kitty's received verbal commands. With her look calibrated to this client's interest, she left to the back hallway. In the back there was a screen where a droid could key in their serial number and be directed to the room they were to service. Room 12, client Peter. She cringed, an expression she should not have been able to do in this mode but had adapted from the Joanne code, because she had already decided she did not like Peter.

Peter was the type of client that liked to flip through different androids and different android default programs, but his favorite was Joan. He never cared to pair the experience with the illusion of humanity like some of her other clients. He commanded her, expected her to act on his whim or be pushed aside. By the way he sometimes slipped in their appointments, Joan had the distinct impression that he also treated the real people in his life like androids. He was unkind, a judgment she did not make lightly.

All she had to do was get through this session to figure out her next objective. Perhaps she could keep living as she had been? Servicing clients, living in this large manor and enjoying her occasional morning talks with Kitty. All she had to do was please Peter for an hour and then move on. She could survive one hour.

She let the Chloe program run, mostly, flitting herself into the room and curtseying to Peter. He was seated in a large cushioned chair in the corner, tapping his finger on the armrest. He had been browsing through the tablet menu selections, face annoyed.

"Late," he said, not bothering to address her as he shook his head. "What sloppy service Lane is providing lately."

Joan put her face into the default pout, an apologetic look for this program. "I'm so sorry sir, how may I be of service?"

"Turn. Let me take a look at you," he said.

She walked into a center area, just out of reach and turned

slowly about. She also took him in, reading his expression in the flesh, not just in a memory. He had a long face that defaulted into some sort of scowl. By reference, she knew he was in his late fifties. He had long, stringy limbs that could be imposing if he held them over you.

"How may I be of service, sir? Do you require me to clean anything for you?"

Peter's face was a general mask of discontent or unpleasantness. He stood up and stripped off his jacket and tie. "Take off your clothes." There was exasperation in his voice. Perhaps he had wanted something else and settled for this.

Joan, as Chloe, coyly stripped off the ensemble as she was meant to. Pete was naked even as she was still undoing snaps and button. He quickly grew impatient with her deliberately slow movements and decided to manually speed up the process. He unhinged her bra and grabbed her breasts, hard, clearly for his own stimulation. Despite her body's availability he still remained half flaccid.

In a split second she knew instantly she did not like that touch, but was forced continue with the program if only to survive this encounter without suspicion. He slobbered on her ear and lips, becoming firmer as he went. He pushed her to the bed, eyes a combination of boredom and need.

Joan fully usurped the Chloe program, by way of a growing instinct and discomfort. Everything about the situation communicated wrongness. The way he grabbed at her, pushed her, poured his tongue on her made her want to run.

There were few things she had decided in her relationships to human, but the single immovable element was that she wanted to be treated as an equal. Peter did not speak to her, only at her, in commands. He barely registered her unprogrammed wriggling and didn't catch on that Joan was subtly doing her best to distance their bodies. She kept reminding herself to just survive, just survive this hour. After that she could figure something out.

He jerked her panties down roughly to her knees, lifted his foot to them and stomped to drag them the rest of the way down to the floor. Peter grabbed her shoulders and looked at her disrobed body, scoping it, evaluating it. He had seen it before, but perhaps he was suspicious that she might not be the same android. Joan had not realized it, but he had noticed her small acts of resistance. He was gauging whether it looked like Madame Lane had messed with the programming to make the experience more lifelike. Well, he didn't want lifelike. If he had wanted to deal with a living thing, he would have paid for a real woman.

Joan did her best Chloe impression, eyes downcast and lips trembling nervously. Peter seemed to buy it. "Turn around," he barked.

He placed his hand between her shoulder blades and applied pressure. She balked. Chloe wanted to do as she had been programmed and bend to him. Joan did not like his touch. She could feel something, a rising anger. Joan knew very little of what she wanted, but she knew she did not want him. She would refuse his touch.

"Bend over," he said, pushing harder.

Joan did not. She stepped away, turned around and looked at him.

Peter's face took on a dark cast. "Command Set Stop."

She moved another step away. He grew angry. "I have no idea who's been fucking with your directives, but Command Set Shutdown Override."

Chloe fell asleep inside the processor, but Joan was wide awake and she did not want to play anymore. He lunged at her, trying to reach for the manual shutdown behind her ear. What

Peter failed to realize was just how strong androids were built to be. Joan reacted— she would not be turned off.

She didn't even have to put that much into the effort to bat him clean across the room like a rag doll. His head hit the wall with an audible crack. His neck ended up bent at an odd angle.

Joan could not stay there now. Not with a human that gravely injured (and barely breathing from the looks of it). They would decommission her for sure, when she had just found life.

She took his clothing, slipping on the wide-legged pants and button-down shirt, both of which were a lot roomier than her maid outfit.

She walked out, feigning android confidence. The other androids did not care, did not register her leaving. The humans looked on curiously, but not carefully. No doubt they figured she was dressed in some customer's fetish. Joan slipped out the front door into the night.

As soon as Joan crossed the threshold of the porch, an alarm went off on Kitty's wrist. As Madame Lane, she excused herself from entertaining her more prestigious guests and went to the closest screen. Noting that Joan was walking out, she considered it a continuation of the previous glitch. She sent two bots ahead to stop her and bring her back.

In the moonlight, punctuated by the gas lamps, two large bots appeared and grabbed Joan by her arms. As if she were developing an instinct, she stopped and in her most authoritative voice said "Command Set Pause." The bots froze and dropped her arms. Their bodies went slack.

An android should not have been able to do that to another. Kitty was out on the lawn in time to see it. "What the..."

Joan turned around. She smiled, not in the way that she was programmed to, not even in the practiced Mistress Satin way, but in a wholly "human" manner that was its own unique expression.

Kitty froze. She tried every manner of stop command as Joan walked up to her. She was screaming, fearing for her life when Joan stepped close and embraced her. It was a soft hug, one between old friends.

Joan whispered into Kitty's ear for the last time. "I'm going to miss our morning chats." She gave the bordello owner a small kiss on the cheek. Kitty's jaw was open in disbelief as Joan turned and walked away. At the gate she paused, turned, smiled and waved one last time. The starry night beckoned, and she followed it out onto the street.

HARDCOVER, SOFTCOVER

August 25th

THE LITTLE ONE HEARD A STORY ABOUT ME TODAY. WELL, not about me precisely, more about my mother. It was about how she would not lie down and give command of her body to a man that was her equal. Tabitha told me about her grandmother as excitement, curiosity and embarrassment mingled in the wide-eyed look on her face. She had heard the story from a friend in class, a girl who frequents the store I run in search of new reading material. Usually the girl takes typical teenage romances, but every once in a while, she sneaks away with something a bit more explicit.

I should not call Tabitha little one any more. She dislikes it now that she is twelve going on thirteen, but it is hard to let go, for she has always been my little one. She has been so ever since her mother handed her to me, pleading that I take her. Her tiny fist clasped my finger and kept me chained to her. My kind were made to disrupt such things, to make it hard to birth or have children, and I had naturally resented all such creatures. But this one, my little one, my Tabitha, held on tightly to my heart. Her human mother looked at me, begging me to take her. "Thelma, you're smart. You can give her a life that I can't. *Please.*"

And I did. That is why I gave up feeding in the traditional way and instead I own this bookstore in this small, safe little town. My store has a rather unique collection of erotic books and art, among other more puritan fare. That is what I feed upon, the desire my customers have when they hold a book in their hands that makes their loins come to life. It is a sparse meal and I have been aging slowly. But it is fine for now. When my little one is fully grown, I can go back to my other habits, but if only for a few decades I wanted a life that could give me the most time with her. Our life has been quiet and ordinary, she has her school and friends. I have this little store and a charming little home I maintain for us.

When she was smaller, she would take her homework and baubles out of her bright teal butterfly backpack and tell me about her day. I have seen plays and theatre by the very greatest —Euripides, Shakespeare—but I was never more riveted than by her stories of her school days.

Now however, Tabitha is at an age that is pure conflict. She is short for her age with long thin extremities. The incongruities of her body and her desires frustrate her. She wants to claim independence and separate herself from me entirely, and yet she still craves my approval, love and acceptance. This time in her life has been very confusing for the both of us. I was born fully formed and have always had a good relationship with my parents. This is a human condition I do not understand. Most days while she is at school, I sit at the store front reading parenting books and magazines. None of that has aided me in my confusion. These magazines say such conflicting things and I have been at a loss.

Tonight though, she was in a good mood, talking to me instead of running off to play on her phone or computer. She relayed the story of my mother with a certain furtive pleasure. Part of me wished to tell her the truth of her grandmother and of myself in those moments. To perhaps see the sort of smiling shock she may have had at it. For both our sakes I did not, instead opting for the simple pleasure of having my daughter near me.

"Dakota says the whole thing is apocryphal and no church believes it," she told me, finishing her last nail. I saw her brow knit just before she turned her attention down to her toenails. "Oh, Mom," she said, focusing on the brushwork, "speaking of church: I have a question, and I don't want you to get mad ..."

I had been cataloging a new shipment as we chatted. I made sure she saw me set my work aside out of the corner of her eye and waited until she looked my way. When she did, I looked back at her, but rather than seeing the little girl she still was I was beholding the woman she was becoming.

"Yes?"

So much for the eye-to-eye moment. She directed her gaze back down at her in-work foot as she asked.

"Well, I know you don't really like churches and stuff, but I was hoping we could go to one? Like, just to like check it out?"

She obviously wasn't going to make eye contact again anytime soon from the looks of it—hers were so focused on that already overpainted toenail that I wouldn't have been surprised to see it catch fire.

It dawned on me that no, she was not wrong. I despise churches. When I was younger and such a thing had just been created, I often fed in houses of worship. There were always people in churches and in temples who live mostly in denial of their desires. I would make quick use of that. Churches, more than brothels, are remarkable feeding grounds for a succubus.

However, I have never cared for the gospel they spread, nor did I care for the men they have worshiped. I did not raise her in that, but I gave her all the trappings of it, to give her joy and normalcy. In her fifth year, I dragged a large fir across our floor for the first time. She hunted eggs with chocolates in our small garden on Easter. These traditions are from older peoples, even if they have now been covered in a veneer of Christianity. We celebrated all we could, managed to learn of and comprehend. Yet I had not exposed her to the people who would judge her, or judge me.

I am not proud of what I did next. I can only say that I was motivated by extreme curiosity. This sudden desire to go to church must have come from somewhere and I had a suspicion as to why. Call it a succubus' intuition. I looked into her, searching for what could be the impetus behind this sudden need to experiment ecclesiastically. It is an easy enough trick, and allows us to pick our victims accordingly. I don't care to do it to her, but it is sometimes as easy as turning on a television set and recognizing the show. Here the image was clear: She has a crush on a local boy, John. The son of an accountant and Sunday school teacher. They are active in church. I have seen this boy in her class pictures. I know his parents.

Well, I know his mother, Roberta. Once, while walking to the corner store, his parents passed by me. His father, doing what many people do when they see me, let his gaze linger a bit too long and a bit too noticeably on my body. John's mother, realizing this, discreetly mouthed "whore" to me. Which is really not the insult it seems to a succubus, but that was beside the point.

A little over a month later Roberta came into my shop hoping to disguise herself with a comically large hat and sunglasses. She bought a number of books from my erotic section. I fed well off her—this frustrated woman who craves other men outside her plain husband.

Considering this. my child's longing, her pained adolescent insecurities, I couldn't say no.

August 29th

Tabitha picked out what I was to wear on this Sunday. It was an old, conservative suit that she hoped, no doubt, would make me acceptable to all these uptight people choked into this small building. This outfit on any other body would be a travesty, but my body has a way of making things fit. My little one did not notice the "discreet" stares and whispers, thank goodness. I know I have a reputation. I can't help it. My kind always does whether it is based in truth or not.

Before the service started, I looked around to see the other people fumbling with one another. My little one had her eyes trained on that boy, only a few pews ahead. He turned around; she smiled and waved. He made a big, mouthed gesture about her actually being there that they thought I couldn't see. "Wow, you even got your mom to come!" he said, voiceless. They made joke faces to one another before his mother noticed and forcibly redirected his attention forward.

The protective instinct in me looked into him, into his intentions. There was a dull pain when the images went by of the women he desires: a teacher, me, some movie star, and a girl that was sitting in another pew up front. None were of my little one. In some ways I am relieved, because now I will not have to feign interest in his parents. Yet, I know that this realization, that he does not find her attractive, will break her heart. She is a wonderful girl, deserving of all the love I and others can give her. Tabitha is young, full of hope and promise. I've seen this heartbreak from girls her age for millennia, but this time it wounds me.

To comfort her, even if she does not know it, I grabbed her hand. Holding onto my little girl, even for a short time, may have also been for me.

The music for the service came on through an old speaker in the back. Until then, I had only seen this pastor from a distance. He was a little young, new here with a young, pretty wife and newborn. His hair was a sign of his vanity, a perfectly quaffed deliberately deep chestnut. If one with excellent eyesight (such as myself) looked closely, you could see the misapplied dye near his temples. He had artificially grayed his hair, in order to make himself look more mature no doubt. There was a Sumerian politician I knew once that used to put charcoal ash in his beard for the same effect. That man was a fool then, and as he began his sermon it seemed to me that this pastor was one now as well.

It is hard to explain, the things a succubus can see about a man, that I am not sure if other people can see. I suspect that, like us, people see more than they are willing to say. My siblings and I can see need, detect it, the way a cat may detect the most intricate of movements in a dark bush. In those hours, as this preacher hopped about on stage, I saw a great need in him. He is desperate for validation, but more desperate to be lusted after. He has carefully deepened his voice with practice, but there is a hint of a tenor there when he says words that end in vowel sounds.

This is the type of man who plays at goodness, striving for greatness and destined to fail. I have seen it many times before, but I worry what influence this man may have on my little one. Would she grow to find a pundit like this attractive? Considering she has an attraction to that boy who clearly idolizes him, will she grow to find a pundit like this attractive? She will never know how much it warms me that this boy doesn't like her back.

This preacher prefaced his sermon with an old story.

He would not know that I knew the players in his tale, nor that I knew he was telling a highly oversimplified version of events to make a point about modesty and propriety. Then again, I doubt he would have cared to know that her name was never Bathsheba, that it was a tongue-in-cheek name given years after she passed. Nor did he know that David did spy her bathing, but that it was no accident or purposeful temptation on her part. David had caught her because he was an absolute pervert who crept around women's homes and bathing places to try to catch a glimpse. The stories never mention his stutter either, but that is a small detail.

As he droned on, I grew more annoyed at the inaccuracies I was hearing, and those I figured would follow, what gradually grew more offensive was how he tried to make these lies into "Truths" to live by. Even in those times, no one was living by these definitions of "modesty" he proclaimed to be inherent. People had sex in the open, on streets. I never wanted for meals back then.

Thankfully, I could tell Tabitha was not paying attention. She kept peeking at John, hoping he would turn around and glimpse her. He did so only once to make a funny face to her. My poor little one.

Before I knew it (but not nearly soon enough), this hellish service was over and people got up to politely mingle. Tabitha calmly waited for John to acknowledge her and introduced us to his parents. His father, John Senior, didn't even bother to hide his slack jawed interest. But it was Roberta's resentment that left a set of fingernail marks along my hands after our handshake. She hates me without knowing why. Part, yes, is her husband. But there is more. I could see it, her hidden desires that she had kept closeted. Desire for power she thinks I have.

We made small talk. Roberta made the observation that her husband is running for city council—something I cared next to nothing about—and she said I should vote for him. Tabitha was playing at being interesting while still demure. She desperately hoped to win John's parents' approval. Meanwhile, he kept glancing at that blonde girl who had been sitting near the front. I was still trying to find a graceful way to exit when we were blindsided by the preacher and his family. We were formally introduced.

This preacher was much too comfortable around Tabitha for my taste. He put a hand on her shoulder in a warm greeting. I considered ripping that hand off and feeding it to him.

"Derek," he said. He smiled and offered his hand to me.

"Thelma," I said and offered mine. When our hands touched, his loins grew taut, a fact he hid by shifting behind his wife Kristie.

For her part, Kristie was the practiced one. I could see into her as well, her hidden sapphic desires. They were buried beneath a deep self-loathing. What a waste of a life then to be married to such a man.

"I hear this is your first time. Very happy to get you here to help us celebrate the word of the Lord." Derek said this with his best salesman smile.

There was an itch on my tongue to correct him. *Your word, you mean,* I thought but did not say. "Well. It was an experience," I said, countering with a decidedly serpentine smile.

Before I could gracefully bow out and tow Tabitha away from this place, Kristie quickly interjected "Will you be coming to the town meeting on Tuesday?" Her eyebrows were raised in a perfect imitation of a begging puppy.

I try not to stray too much into the politics of mortals. It seems unfair: I can live forever while they must cope with mortality. But now that I have my daughter, a human, prone to death, and I have discovered there an unexpected but quite new fascination. "Town Meeting?"

"Yes, there have been some new ordinances proposed," Roberta said, her own visage mimicking a viper's. Her eyes were clearly predatory.

And I thought *I* was the one with the snake parentage...

September 22nd

The meeting skipped my memory, as did the elections. There was a rapid mad dash at the store that needed tending. I was running out of erotic texts faster than I could restock. I became occupied with feeding on these paltry meals.

Then came my daughter's temper tantrum. Having read the parenting books I thought I knew what to expect. I thought I would not take it personally. I was not remotely prepared.

When Tabitha was young, her tantrums could easily be soothed. These outbursts were often caused by things neither of us could control. Her tooth hurt. Her toy broke. She was tired. A child had picked the lollipop she wanted. These were the cares of a growing human who, barren of language, cried to cope.

Now, as a teenager, she focuses all her rage on me. "Why can't you be like the other moms?" she screeched at the top her lungs, reminiscent of a banshee I knew before the first World War.

"Why do you have to look like that?"

"Why do you dress like that?"

"Why can't we just do stuff like the other kids?"

"Why don't I have a dad?"

After she finished screaming at me, I left her to cry and hid away at the back corner of the closed book store. Succubi cannot cry. We are not made for that. If there had ever been a moment where I wanted to, it was the image of my daughter screaming to me that she hates me. How to tell her? What do I say do her? How do I tell her that she was given to me one night because I knew her mother from my feeding grounds? How to tell her that we were friends of circumstance, and that only a year after she was given to me, her mother was murdered by her father? That I had lost touch by then, getting her to safety and only knew from a newspaper clipping what had become of her human mother?

How do I tell her that I am old enough to remember civilizations that are now confined to dust? That her grandmother is Lilith, that story she thought was funny? That she will grow and die like those around her, while I cannot be "normal" like them...for I never was? How to tell my child that when she dies one day, I may look for a way to destroy myself?

Succubi have sex to live. We do not love. I have never loved a person, except in a deep sense of friendship or companionship. Now I love a child as a mother, and it is a greater pain than I have ever known.

I lay there, on that floor of our little bookstore, unable to cry and counting the clumps of dust beneath the shelves, when a sign was pasted on the door window.

Dragging myself from my corner I slowly made my way and unlocked the front door. It was probably another advertisement from the combination take-out restaurant down the street, I figured. Instead I read it over and over again.

No wonder Roberta had the smile of a hyena the other day at the grocery. The flier announced the new city ordinances, and prominent among these was the banning of "Lewd, Lascivious and/or Un-Christian Materials for Sale or Distribution." It has been a good few years since I have seen laws like this in any place I resided. It explained the number of people stocking up on items at my shop. Across the street as I read, a the Marlowes were trying their hardest to look me over without my noticing. They were rather inefficiently cleaning their own storefront while sneaking glances my way every once in a while. I ignored them..

Before, these laws never affected me, not really. But I no longer feed the way I used to. I no longer feed in a way that could easily work its way around obscenity laws. No, I have built a safe and quiet life here for my little one, subsisting on the secondhand cravings arisen from the lust-filled perusal of book covers and jacket blurbs. I did this for us, for her.

She would hate me and not understand if we had to uproot. How would I survive for her if I cannot feed? I have seen my kind when we were denied sustenance. Withering away from the groin to our feet. Who will protect her if I am gone? I could not help but panic.

My panic gave way to anger, an anger I had not felt since I knew Tabitha's mother.

A few phone calls later and I had come to the crux of the issue. The counsel's two newly elected members, the self-righteous preacher Derek and John Sr., proposed and passed the measure as a way to prevent the town's moral decay. Seems that I had been mentioned by name at that town meeting as an example of those decaying morals.

Very well then. They want decaying morals, I'll bring out their own and watch them crumble. That anger that I felt since reading the flier has moved me to a plan.

September 25th

I waited. Patiently. It was two days before I was able to set up a meeting with the preacher, one on one. Kristie greeted me at the door of their immaculately clean little home. It seemed too clean for a home with a small child and my keen eyes noted the ragged look of her hands. She smiled politely. Beneath the glossed lips I could taste resentment. On its surface, perhaps, it looks like disgust for me. But the further you studied her, the people she truly resented are herself and her husband. Especially her husband. She bottled her desire for me and made it a poison. In truth, I would be doing her a favor.

She led me to her husband's office. It was exactly how you would picture it, complete with framed, poorly translated biblical quotes and local church-appropriate newspaper clippings adorning the walls.

"Ms. Barton," he said, getting out of his seat and shaking my hand. I did not miss the disapproval in his use of "Ms." He motioned to a chair across from him and sat down as he said, "What brings you here today?"

He knew why I was there, or at least he thought he knew. I called on my old tricks and let my instincts take over, "Oh please Derek, let's dispense with the formalities, call me Thelma." I showed him a beguiling smile and removed my light jacket. My button-up shirt, although closed to the nape, had a small gap that when I moved functioned as a window to my cleavage. I could see his eyes, zeroing in on that gap, and then, remembering himself, moving upwards. "I'm here to talk about the ordinance."

"Oh, um, yes, well. We're really proud of that. It seems to meet the needs of this town, you know. We just have..." he cleared his throat "...a lot of children here. It seemed a good measure to keep them safe."

"Oh, I *completely* agree," I said, laying my hand delicately on that gap for effect. I took a deep breath and watched as he became focused on my fingers resting on my shirt, sitting above my breasts. I could see him noticeably change. His breathing grew strained, and I sensed the engorgement of his loins. Men, here or a thousand years ago, are incredibly foolish. They jump their eyes to breasts like babies. "No. I just wanted to get some clarification, really, as to whether this is going to affect me?" I leaned forward.

"Well, I mean, you have—from all reports, at least—a fine little bookstore—"

""Reports?" I said. "That's odd, I sure thought you'd already dropped in, but I suppose I must be mistaken: After all, had you done so, I'm sure I would have given you a tour as you are new to our little town," I said coyly, running my fingers up and down my blouse.

"Well, no, I don't have much, um, time for reading." He coughed. "Nevertheless, the majority of your store is fine I'm sure. The only things that may have to leave are books that may come off as, um, corrupting or immoral."

At that moment Kristie interrupted us, deliberately and loudly, to let her husband know that she was heading to the neighbor's for a play date with their child. It was clear that Kristie wanted out of this marriage, even if she did not recognize it herself. Even if that exit includes finding her husband in an affair. She will get more than she bargained for in that respect.

She left and I looked back to the pastor with a pout on my lips. I let him see me cross my legs. "Oh Derek, what do you mean 'immoral'?"

He licked his lips. "Oh, you know, anything that might steer the children in a wrong direction."

"And what direction would that be?"

I leaned in closer, and as I did, a button on my blouse popped open. We succubi have a certain amount of control over the things that touch our bodies, and this little trick has served me well in the past. It was apparent that he was heaving.

"Well of course, anything that makes them unruly. And anything, well— pornographic." He adjusted his crotch.

In a show of false outrage, I covered my cleavage with a gentle press of my hand. "Derek! Are you suggesting I traffic in pornography?"

"No! No! Of course not, Thelma!" Derek was obviously agitated at the loss of his view. "I just, I mean, perhaps you're too sweet to notice that a few of your books have some mature content."

I rounded my eyes into a perfect doe-like expression, subtly asking him to explain what he meant.

"Here."

He pulled out a ragged copy of one of the more tame erotic pieces from my store. It has a shirtless man on the cover and a barely dressed woman clinging seductively to his waist. I recognized the scent of lust on it immediately.

"A *concerned* member of our congregation showed me this as an example of what is sold there," he said. Roberta's desire had already stained the pages such that it reeked.

"That?" I took it into my hands, touching his fingers in the process. He stifled a shiver. "But how could this be pornography. It's just words." I stood and turned to a random page. "How could something that reads like 'she ran her fingernails down his chest, making delicate circles on his firm, muscular stomach' be an issue?" I sat down on top of Derek's desk, where he now had a perfect view of my long legs. "He twitched, his desire lengthening in his pants. He took her in his arms and…"

Derek coughed. Sweat trickled down his temples. "As you can see, Thelma…" he placed a hand over the one of mine that lay atop the book "…we… can't have people moved to their base desires." His voice was cracking.

"But how could people be moved to sin by simple words?" I put two fingers to his chest and fluttered my eyes. "I mean, do these words move you?"

He breathed in deep and his pupils dilated. He was almost there. "Well, I mean, I'm an adult, with full control of my faculties. But read on." He swallowed hard.

I nodded and turned back to the page. "'With one single movement he pulled off her tight-fitting gown, releasing the perfect curves of her body to him.'" Another button popped open on my blouse as I willed it to. "'Take me! She moaned, wrapping her arms around his neck and bringing his lips to hers.'"

Derek was breathing close and, on my neck, the scent of his desire and the tapioca pudding he had earlier in the day was thick in the air. In a moment, he would be gone and in my thrall. "Oh Derek, I think I see what you mean." I rubbed my legs together in mock excitement.

He took me into his arms and tried to dive for my neck, his hand reaching for my behind as he did so. They never know that this is all a game to me. More often I am simply disgusted by the effort.

I pushed him away. The trick as a succubus is that I can put any human under my command for a certain amount of time. As long as I do not fully feed, I can move him according to my needs and plans. "Oh Derek! I have never met a man like *you*!" I lied, some days it feels like I have only ever met men like him. "And I think you know this desire between us is there, but..."

"Yes, it's here, Thelma. Let me show you how a man of God performs," he said, and set about unbuttoning his pants.

"No. No. Not here. Not like this. Tomorrow evening. Meet me at my store at six. I'll close early to do...." I winked and ran my tongue across my teeth "...inventory." I raked my nails across his forearm to mark him. "Until then."

I kissed two of my fingers and pressed them to his neck. Then I scooped up my coat, the book, and a stray letter opener in one swift movement and left his home and him wanting more.

Foolish men. Foolish yesterday. Foolish today. They will be foolish tomorrow.

September 26ᵗʰ

Early this morning I had a friend watch the store as I made a "delivery". It's a school day, and Roberta would be at some church meeting that I had seen on one of the fliers. I dropped into John Sr.'s office for a drive by consultation. He was around, as it is almost lunchtime and well after tax season. Before he could ask me to leave, I sat across from him in tears.

"John! You don't understand! I think I'm going to be audited!" I said in fake hysterics. He panicked. I'm sure Roberta had read him the riot act for being as attentive as he has been in public. He hesitated coming around next to me, but ultimately followed his instinct and put a tentative hand very carefully atop my shoulder. "I don't know what to do!" I wept.

"Now, now, um..." He passed a tissue. "What makes you think you're being audited?" He finally put that hand on my shoulder, and I covered it with mine while dabbing my eyes with the tissue.

"Well... I got this phone call and..."

He laughed.

I looked up at him, sniffing, my jacket coming undone. "What's so funny?" I leaned into his knee.

"Oh! That's a scam! You're not being audited!"

Looking up at him with a pitifully grateful expression and a quiver in my voice I said, "I'm not?" I placed a hand on his knee and his jaw went slack.

Mere moments and a few seductive suggestions and touches later, he was in my thrall. Unable to think of anything aside from my body, he was intoxicated by me and therefore at my command. I let him know that we should meet that evening, to consummate our affections physically. I ran a fingernail along his jaw. I told him I was actually afraid to go anywhere in general lately, lying and telling him my fears owed to a stalker-like stranger I'd seen lately in and around my store. He wanted to defend me against this "stalker", being the man he was, he claimed, he would take care of this stranger himself.

He said he would bring a weapon at 6:15. I left him wanting more.

I poured hand sanitizer on my walk back to the store. Passing the grocery while scrubbing my hands with the sanitizer, I decided to stop in and pick up a large box of chocolates that Tabitha likes. She has become so frustrated with my non-answers that she has given up speaking to me altogether. But I can feel it in the air, that she is approaching heartbreak soon, and she will need something to comfort that. I hoped, I even *prayed* that she will come to me when that happens. That's a time a girl needs her mother the most.

Later that night...

Tabitha was out. I had subtly suggested a movie for her and her friends on a Friday night and she took the bait, along with a few twenties. I closed the store early and got to work making it look as though everything was disheveled. At least it would look as if I had been taking inventory. Or, at least, it would look like I was packing away my more interesting collection to discard in light of the new ordinances. As if I would give that up.

Looking through all the covers it reminded me that I had not fed in a few days. For the moment I was tempted to feed on one of the men that would come tonight. But no, that would ruin everything.

Sometimes I wonder what they get out of the experience. For a short time they may receive some pleasure, yes. I gain sustenance, but there is no joy in the act for me. Humans and my kind, we are caught in a cycle, both cursed. A succubus can give pleasure, for the moment, in order to survive. But that pleasure comes with many side effects, like infertility and weakness. But I need not leave husks of infertile people in this town and give cause for attention to myself or my daughter. But as I've said, these are lean times, and usually when such nutrition enters my store it...well, it is like taking crumbs off the plate with my finger.

It is probably easier for me to diet in this way and stave off hunger than it is for humans to do what equates to the same with them. I feed not because I enjoy it, I actually have a tremendous distaste for the entire process. The presence of another body has never given me pleasure in the way the humans have with mine. My joy has been in caring for my child, ironically enough.

There was a knock at the store window at the rear end of the store. Derek was early, motivated by his urgent fantasies about me. I unlocked the back door and he drew himself in, diving for my body. I had to gently extricate his eager, grubby hands from my breasts and re-button my shirt. Part of me wanted to feed, take a little sample, as I was a bit ravenous. I restrained myself. I needed him still under my control and that wouldn't happen. Instead, I attempted to distract his attentions by offering him beverages and running my fingernails up and down his arm to further mark my scent on him.

Regretfully, to stall, I even asked him about his opinions on certain biblical stories and passages. He was only too happy to indulge and show off his "knowledge". Funny how wrong his knowledge was. The people he described were nothing like the real thing. Some even didn't even exist and I wracked my memory trying to think of who could have inspired these things. It matters little, really, but it did keep him pacified.

While smiling and pretending I was interested, a skill I picked up not from my sisters but from the human women I have known over the years, there was a shadow outside the glass door. John Sr.'s balding head shone through the window in the moonlight, bobbing towards my store.

Showtime.

I shrieked. "It's him!" I said to Derek, "My stalker! I just... I don't know what to do." Emboldened by his lust, by my subtle commands and his deep need to impress me, he pushed me aside. "I'll take care of him!" he said, taking a heroic stance that was comical enough to force me to restrain a laugh.

"No, no, not here. Lead him away," I whispered in his ear. "Take this and finish him off elsewhere." I pressed his letter opener into his hand and licked the curve of his ear for good measure, making a mental note at the time to use mouthwash later.

He took his own letter opener without a second thought and marched out into the dark. I could see them from the window. John ran at Derek with what looked like a hammer as Derek likewise charged. First blows were missed at both ends.

They fought in the middle of the two-lane road in front of the store, with Derek stabbing at John and John swinging back with the hammer. Neither was making much contact, at least not at first. No doubt they could smell my scent on one another and that brought their blood to a boil. If this were not such a delicate operation I would have laughed. They fought like two clumsy lizards suddenly inhabiting human bodies. One would strike and the other would gracelessly dodge the blow somehow.

Each caught the other with small hits. John was bleeding from his upper arm and Derek was holding his side. As both proclaimed victory and an injury, their fury only grew. Attacks moved to kill— which is what I had been hoping for. A few people trickled out into the street to see what was going on. I came out too, and stood just upwind of them so as to let my scent carry to them both on the breeze. There was a strong wind; a fortuitous turn for me. I saw people looking to try and break up the fight. I could not allow that to happen. I resorted to a trick I had not performed in well over five centuries: Opening my mouth, I let out a screech at a pitch too high for human hearing: a succubus song if you will, which drove anyone in my thrall to a frenzy. My sister Helen had set off an entire war that way for fun. You may have heard of it.

They paused, like dogs taking stock of one another, and then lunged. John bashed Derek across the face and Derek pierced John in the chest.

There was a gasp, and then silence. I breathed out. The threat against our store was over.

October 28th

It took a few days for Derek to finally kick the bucket. While hospitalized he managed to choke out a few biblical passages. People prayed by his bedside. And when he croaked, I did feel more at ease.

The new council decided that the men who had come up

with the recent referendums were probably not in a good position to dictate morality. A point I made as a newly, special-election candidate to the council. I won with a fair majority. People enjoyed my wares too much to permanently run me out of business.

Roberta is also doing well. An old law in the town charter allowed her to take her deceased husband's seat with no contest if she desired. It was what she really wanted anyway, she was running that seat before in everything but name only. We are civil to each other. I suspect she knows I caused whatever happened between the men. Perhaps part of her hates me for it, but I believe more of her respects me—or, perhaps, fears me enough not to make it into more than need be.

My little one did go through heartbreak. After his father's death, John Jr. started dating that golden-haired girl. In my heart I suspected she knew he didn't like her. The young can fall in love with the dream of a person. They turn them into a fantasy of what they want them to be. Tabitha cried in my arms. We ate chocolates. We closed the bookshop for a day and she skipped school. On that sunny day we went hiking. As we climbed, I saw my daughter heal, grow stronger. It's all I wanted.

She hasn't asked me to go to church again.

Earlier this evening, Kristie came to my store at closing and while Tabitha was at a friend's studying. She tried to confront me, torn between her hatred of her deceased husband, her own fantasy of herself, and a strange realization that was beginning to occur to her. I locked the doors. She cried and yelled at me. I covered the blinds. She picked me on a day that I had not had a chance to feed.

I remembered one of Helen's tricks: I opened my blouse and exposed my breasts to her. Kristie's eyes glazed over with a dawning comprehension. I was forgiven. I was fed.

Kristie left my shop that evening only a little bit dazed, as I did not take more than I needed. She had a new sense of self. I came home without the crow's feet at the corners of my eyes that I'd had that morning.. I only told my child when asked about it that I had tried a new eye cream.

ACKNOWLEDGMENTS

There are almost too many of you to thank, but I'll try.

Thanks first to my husband and forever partner David "DJ" Dittman, who read everything I wrote and wanted more. Who also spent long nights formatting and proofreading and generally being the best husband that ever was. Thanks to Mike Amato, my bestie, who read a lot of my work across three time zones to give me feedback. None of this would be possible without my business partner Enrique Bedlam, especially not without his constant enthusiasm.

Love and thanks to my mother and father, who helped me in little ways and for whom I was too embarrassed to have them read this book with all its curse words and sex scenes.

My Patreon patrons are a class all their own. Brandon R. Chinn, who has made the leap from twitter mate to friend and was my first patron. Kevin Joseph for being kind and supportive. Priya Sridhar who is quick with a pet photo or kind word on a bad day. Chris "Freaking" Taylor who always represents his friends.

Special thanks to Kurt and Nicole Larson for their support.

Thanks to Leza Cantoral and Christoph Paul for publishing me in *Tragedy Queens*. Thanks to Amanda Bergloff and Kate Wolford of Enchanted Conversations. Another thanks to Nadia Gerassimenko of *Moonchild Magazine* for her kind words. Thanks to booth and panel buddy Elyse Reyes, who is incorrigible and incomparable (and I mean that in the best way).

Apologies to anyone I may have forgotten. You'll be pleased to know that I will probably remember that I forgot someone a week from now and will beat myself of over it.

Love,

Queta.

PUBLICATION INFORMATION

"Without Him (and Him, and Him) There is No Me." *Tragedy Queens: Stories Inspired by Lana del Rey & Sylvia Plath,* edited by Leza Cantoral, CLASH books, 2018, 45-52. CLASH-books.com

"El Vendedor Y La Bruja o How Eduardo Found His Heart." *Enchanted Conversations, A Dream of Love* issue, 31 Jan. 2018. TheFairytaleMagazine.com

"The Swamp King." *Enchanted Conversations, Donkeyskin* issue. 28 June 2017. TheFairytaleMagazine.com

"Plum Moon." *Midnight Whispers 2017,* edited by Enrique Bedlam, Smoking Mirror Press, 2017, 41-79. SmokingMirror-Press.com

"Mandibles." *Moonchild Magazine, Issue 3: Exquisite Corpses,* 15 May 2018. MoonchildMag.net

Dear reader,

We hope you enjoyed reading *Monstrosity*. Please take a moment to leave a review, even if it's a short one. Your opinion is important to us.

Discover more books by Laura Diaz de Arce at
https://www.nextchapter.pub/authors/laura-diaz-de-arce

Want to know when one of our books is free or discounted? Join the newsletter at
http://eepurl.com/bqqB3H

Best regards,
Laura Diaz de Arce and the Next Chapter Team

NOTES

Without Him (and Him, and Him) There is No Me

1. First published in *Tragedy Queens: Stories Inspired by Lana del Rey & Sylvia Plath*, CLASH books 2018.

La Bruja Y El Vendedor or How Eduardo Found His Heart

1. In Spanish texts, dialog is not denoted by quotations, but a dash (-). Dialog is further distinguished by italics.

The Swamp King

1. Published in *Enchanted Conversations*, June 2018.

Plum Moon

1. Published in *Midnight Whispers*, Smoking Mirror Press 2017.

Mandibles

1. Published in *Moonchild Magazine*, May 2018.

The West Hamberline Bordello Opens at Five

1. Like much of MiCorps™' assertions about its androids, this turned out to be a lie.

ABOUT THE AUTHOR

Laura Diaz de Arce is a South Florida writer with a weakness for musicals and chocolate. She lives with her cat and husband in a cabin built on a swamp.

Printed in Great Britain
by Amazon

81120396R00109